Advance praise for

The Future of White Men
and Other Diversity Dilemmas

"I'm trying to find my way to the great diversity picnic but round and round I go, lost in the forest. Old fears I didn't know were there loom up; old prejudices, old stereotypes, new political (in)correctness tangle my feet, scratch at my good will, obscure the path.

But wait, here comes rescue! The brave and delightful Joan Lester has walked these woods, has tamed these monsters for years. Hallelujah, she knows the way!

Thank you, Dr. Lester, for this wise, compassionate and witty book. I have been waiting for it for a long time."

Ronnie Gilbert, singer, actor, playwright/author

"Lester's sympathetic understanding of the plight of the '25% of the U.S. population—heterosexual white males' sets the tone for her important book: No one is to blame, everyone has something to learn!"

**Lee Nichols, Professor Emeritus,
Communication Studies, California State University**

". . . an excellent guide through the maze of modern relationships to a richer understanding of ourselves and our fellow human beings."

**James C. Hormel, Chairman, Equidex, Inc.,
Board of Managers, Swarthmore College**

"Inspiring, witty, a fresh and essential perspective in the most complex issues to today's world. I loved it."

Nancy K.D. Lemon, Attorney,
UC Berkeley, Boalt School of Law

"In a time when we need to move beyond the rhetoric of diversity issues, this book should be a required text for everyone. Lester makes the issues real. She offers visible examples and practical strategies for addressing the diversity dilemmas of the next decade."

Jamie Washington, Ph.D., Executive Council,
American College Personnel Association

"Provides new inspiration for building a truly diverse America."

Rabbi Sheila Peltz Weinberg,
Jewish Community of Amherst, Massachusetts

". . . a must-read book for all people."

The Reverend Eloise Oliver,
Oakland, California

"In this book, Lester has managed the improbable task of presenting the very serious concerns of diversity, racism, and change, in a funny, witty, and hopeful manner."

Sonia Nieto, Professor, University of Massachusetts,
author of *Affirming Diversity*

"Clear and sensible personal strategies that can move one beyond feelings of guilt, resentment, and paralysis."

Barbara Walker, the country's first Diversity Manager,
Diversity Enterprises

The Future
of White Men
and Other Diversity
Dilemmas

The Future
of White Men
and Other Diversity
Dilemmas

Joan Steinau Lester

Conari Press
Berkeley, CA

Parts of this book have been previously published in *USA Today*, the *Los Angeles Times*, *San Fransicso Examiner*, *Chicago Tribune*, *New Directions for Women*, *Cincinnati Enquirer*, *Fort Worth Star-Telegram*, *Walla Walla Union-Bulletin*, *Arizona Republic*, *Bangor Daily News*, *Hunstville Times*, *Roanoke Times and World-News*, *Kentucky Enquirer*, *Honolulu Advertiser*, *Richmond Times-Dispatch*, *Salt Lake Tribune*, *Fayetteville Observer-Times*, the *Contra Costa Times*, and other newspapers.

"For The White Person Who Wants to Know How to Be My Friend" by Pat Parker from *Movement in Black*, copyright © 1978 by Pat Parker. Reprinted by permission of Firebrand Books, Ithaca, NY.

Signe cartoon, Peres/Arafat Peace Agreement 1992. Reprinted by permission of Cartoonists & Writers Syndicate.

Printed in the United States of America on recycled paper
Cover: Sharon Smith Design; illustration: Mercedes McDonald; handlettering: Lily Lee

ISBN: 0-943233-61-5 (Paperback)

Library of Congress Cataloging-in-Publication Data

Lester, Joan Steinau, 1940-
  The future of white men and other diversity dilemmas / by Joan Steinau Lester.
      p.   cm.
    ISBN 0-943233-61-5 (pbk.) : $9.95
    1. Equality--United States.   2. Pluralism (Social sciences)--United States.   I. Title.   II. Title: Diversity dilemmas.
  HN90.S6L47   1994
  305--dc20
                                                              93-42344
                                                                  CIP

"We may have come in different ships, but we're all in the same boat now."
—Martin Luther King, Jr.

To which wisdom I add only: And some of us were already here . . . but we're all in the same boat now.

The Future of White Men and Other Diversity Dilemmas

Acknowledgments

If I can see over the mountain at all, it is because I stand on the shoulders of giants. Six whom I was fortunate to work with during the years I was developing my ideas were: Ann Mari Buitrago, a friend/mentor from my early twenties, and Karl Niebyl at the New School in New York City; then in my thirties, colleagues Barbara Love, Bailey Jackson and my dissertation director, Bob H. Suzuki, all at the University of Massachusetts, Amherst; and Ricky Sherover Marcuse of Oakland, California. Each was a pioneer in some aspect of diversity work. Each taught me much.

I have also been fortunate to have participated in thinking about diversity—as we've practiced and preached it—with a group of extraordinary training specialists at Equity Institute. Those who have been involved in that learning process with me at some point over the past twelve years are Heru Nefera Amen, Aquila Ayana, Jim Bonilla, Loel Greene, Carole Johnson, Barbara Love, Yeshi Sherover Neumann, Patricia Romney, Beverly Daniel Tatum, Valerie Taylor, Cooper Thompson, and Jamie Washington. It is a gift to have had colleagues such as these.

The Board of Directors and staff of Equity Institute, who have created an institute to support the development of these ideas, are very much a part of this book also. Core board members have been Martha Ackelsburg, Sam Bowles, Ann DeGroot, John Eastman, Jyl Felman, Jean Genasci, Carl Griffin, Lorraine Hart, Barbara Love, Darlene Miller, Daphne Muse, Sonia Nieto, Eleanor Holmes Norton, Maureen Phillips, Betty Powell, Raúl Quiñones-Rosado, Linda Randall, Sontiago Rodriquez, Elaine Seiler, Beverly Daniel Tatum, Sheila Weinberg, Muriel Wiggins, Hazaiah Williams, and Thomas Wolf. My thanks also to past staff members Angela DoCanto and Mei-Ying Wong.

I have had enthusiastic support for my writing from many quarters. In 1991 I was selected as a Windcall Resident, went to Montana on a retreat, and finally had the time to figure out what kind of writing I wanted to do next. I decided to write op-ed newspaper columns: bite-sized, humorous pieces about diversity topics. My thanks to Albie and Susan Wells for their vision in creating this one-of-a-kind residency program for social justice leaders. And thanks to Sid

Hurlburt at *USA Today*, Lynn Ludlow at the *San Francisco Examiner*, and Lynn Wenzel at *New Directions for Women* for their encouragement and publication of so many of my columns.

My friends and family have all been extremely supportive. Andrea Ayvazian, Mary Ann Cofrin and Melinda Shaw, Veronica Dare, Ronnie Gilbert and Donna Korones, Jim Hormel, Ruth King, Patty Ramsey, Eva Schocken, Maxine Wolfe, Morton, Barbara, and Mardi Steinau, and my son and daughter have each lent critical encouragement or had key discussions at various stages of my development as a writer. I especially appreciate the support of my parents as I keep taking new leaps—following in their adventurous footsteps. My friend Donna Korones has my special gratitude for thinking about the book with me from the moment it was a brand-new idea through the final drafts. As do Chandra Kendrix and Carole Johnson, for their encouragement and insights.

And what I have learned from my many manuscript readers! Kosta Bagakis, Arelene Cordero, Donna Nomura Dobkin, Ronnie Gilbert, Diane Goldstein, Eleanor Grier, Jim Hormel, Carole Johnson, Irene Johnson, Chandra Kendrix, Donna Korones, Barry Myles, Yeshi Sherover Neumann, Mardi Steinau, Virna Tintiangco, Tamyra Walz, and Léonie Walker—their comments helped lift these words. Thanks also to Maurice Jourdain-Earl for information on mortgage practices.

I've been blessed with an editor, Mary Jane Ryan, who cares deeply about her society, and took on this project with passion and skill.

I am blessed with all that and more. Carole, my life partner, has supported me every single day for over twelve years with her vision of a better world coming, and me as one of its midwives. The constancy of her love, as well as her insight, never ceases to amaze me. If there is one co-creator, she is it.

Thank you to all I have named, and also to those unnamed whose paths have crossed mine. I hope this book does you proud.

Introduction

Everybody seems to be getting a seat at the table these days. People who once carried the trays are sitting down, people who sat at the foot of the table are now honored guests, and people who took notes at the meetings are now running those meetings. Women, employees in wheelchairs, same-sex partners, men of color, old people, large people. The legal barriers are coming down—and now we all have to get along.

It isn't easy.

Most of us are well intentioned. We're doing our best, trying to do the right thing. Yet when it comes to interacting with people different from ourselves, much of the time we aren't very successful.

This is not the world in which we grew up. Yet here we are, expected to function today—with yesterday's mindset.

So we try to make friends; we try to create equitable environments at work or at school. And we often get blown out of the water. Eventually, we just want to stay in our neighborhoods with everyone else who is pretty much like ourselves.

Somehow, though, we can't get away. The cousin named Gonzales (when our last name is Glenn), the aunt named Weinstein (ours is Wayne)—they keep popping up. Along with our son and his long-time "friend," the daughter who marries "outside the race," or the sister who can't get to a job because the bus in her town still isn't wheelchair accessible. The conflict between groups keeps occurring, right under our noses.

In the past we knew what to expect. White men ran not only the meetings but the country, women raised children (their own and others'), people of color served. Gay men, lesbians, and people with disabilities didn't exist—not in polite company, anyway. Women who married were fired from their jobs. Jews were in separate clubs. Young people were to be seen and not heard. Old people faded away.

And now the rules are changing, right in the middle of our lives. We are all learning—those of us newly seated at the table and those who are having to move over to make a little more room.

This book looks at the diversity dilemmas we all confront in daily life, hopefully providing some new folklore to fall back on for those moments when you wonder, Now what do I say, what do I do?

For instance:

How do you handle the joke—the joke that relies for its humor on a stereotype you'd rather not hear—told by your brother at the all-too-rare family celebration? Or told by your boss?

And what do you say when a co-worker says she doesn't want to be called *Black*, she prefers *African-American*?

Then, just when you've learned to say "African-American" comfortably, how do you react to the man who hears you speak, then says he's African-Caribbean? The term African-*American* excludes his culture, and he's mighty tired of hearing it.

How do you respond to the yoga teacher who asks you to sit "Indian-style"? What, after all, is in a word?

You don't want to mince words, yet you don't want to offend.

Physically challenged, handicapped or *people with disabilities*? It's hard to keep up. And do we really have to?

Or, as a member of an excluded group yourself, what do you do when you see that you still haven't gotten your fair share, and now newfound "minorities" are getting all the attention? Everybody seems to be jumping on the diversity bandwagon.

What do you do if you are a straight, white, middle-class, middle-aged woman who suddenly realizes that all your friends are exactly the same?

What do you do when the search committee turns

up another white male and says there's nobody else out there who is "qualified"?

Or you're a white male who sometimes wonders, amidst all the talk of diversity: Should I be put on the endangered-species list?

You're trying not to make a mistake and you want to be fair. You're under some pressure to reach out. You want to keep your sense of humor and a sense of proportion. Yet you sometimes feel that various groups are overly sensitive. Can't we all just get along?

What do you say when . . . you are alive in the 1990s and the new diversity is everywhere apparent?

You may be afraid of failure or of looking foolish. Afraid of being considered a bigot or a troublemaker. It often seems easier, and safer, to do nothing.

Yet all of this "diversity stuff" isn't going to go away. We are, all of us, going to have to figure out how to sit down together at the welcome table.

I've been fortunate to have had life push me—or perhaps I jumped—into the center of many of these issues during the past thirty years. I got involved in the civil rights movement as a teenager, and a few years later did just what white people were so often afraid white women would do if we "socialized": I married one. A Black man. When it was still illegal in twenty-seven of these United States to do so. And then I did the next worst thing a white woman could do in that situation. Had children.

Shortly afterward, I found out that even in a civil

rights movement for justice, "the position of women in this organization is prone," as one of its leaders said. I thus became one of the many creators of this wave of the women's movement, starting a group in New York and becoming a delegate to the first national Women's Liberation Conference in 1968.

Then, not content to leave trouble alone, in 1981 I chose as my life partner a person to whom it is still illegal to be married. A woman. With whom I've been lucky enough to be partners ever since.

And I can tell just what's coming next. The old ones. We're readying our forces, and I know I'll be right in the middle of it all.

Living my life and observing the lives of others has taught me most of what I know. I learned a few things in school, too, getting a doctorate in multicultural education and teaching at several colleges.

In 1982 I co-founded Equity Institute, with a mission of "turning *isms* into *wasms*." Since then I've been consulting, writing, speaking, and coaching executives on diversity all over the U.S.

We all do our own learning. You will need to take your own risks and make your own mistakes to do yours. My hope is that this book will give you some insights, and some laughter, to ease your way on the road to tomorrow—or really, today.

1

Who Gets a Seat?

Who Gets a Seat at the Table?

We've been playing a long game of musical chairs in the United States. The music has played on for hundreds of years, stopping for a moment every generation when it seemed that everyone had a shot at a seat.

In reality, few players had permanent seats. Yet we got used to playing the game that way. Every time it looked as though there might be a vacant seat, we all ran for it—or wheeled along in our chairs. We got there however we could. And we did just what we were supposed to do in the game of musical chairs: We pushed each other out of the way.

"It's mine. That seat is mine."

"No, I have waited too long. That seat must be for me."

Sometimes one, sometimes another got the empty seat. Sometimes those who already had the permanent seats simply annexed the empty one—after everyone else had a "fair chance."

Every once in a while a group of people said, "The reason we aren't getting any seats isn't because we aren't running fast enough. Or working hard enough. It's the rules of the game."   And finally, massive movements. "The rules need to change."

So for a generation we had one seat on the Supreme Court for an African-American (male). Then for a decade, another seat for a (white) female.

Now the rules have changed again. We don't have just one token seat. Sometimes we have two or three. In more places every year the permanent seats are no longer guaranteed. And the pace is increasing. Every day's newspaper brings a story of a "first"—or a second.

One of our current "seconds" is Supreme Court Justice Ruth Bader Ginsberg. In 1956, when she was a student at Harvard Law School, Dean Erwin Griswold asked each of the nine women in the class how they felt about taking places "earmarked for men." His language revealed his understanding of who occupied the permanent seats and who were the guests.

Nonetheless, Ruth Bader graduated with honors— and couldn't get a job interview. Justice Felix Frankfurter himself is reputed to have asked an aide, "Does she wear skirts? I can't stand girls in pants!" before he refused to interview her.

"In the Fifties," Judge Ginsberg later wrote, "the traditional law firms were just beginning to turn around on hiring Jews. But to be a woman, a Jew and a mother to boot—that combination was a bit too much."

Today there are more seats available. But we have yet to open up all of them, and this gives a sense of scarcity. It isn't only white men who are concerned that they will be pushed aside in the rush to diversity. Each group formerly excluded is also worried that there won't be enough seats to go around.

Blacks versus Gays

Each group wonders whether its concerns will be adequately addressed. For example, there has recently been considerable African-American resentment reported of gay (and before that, of women's) appropriation of the language of the civil rights struggle.

Which raises the question: Is it disrespectful of one human rights movement for another to use its imagery?

This issue comes up in other contexts. Jews sometimes bristle when other disasters are called a Holocaust. "We don't want the word, and therefore our pain, to be watered down."

There are marked differences between the particularities of each group's struggle. Yet, to paraphrase

Jesse Jackson (in the style of Gertrude Stein), discrimination is discrimination is discrimination. Those who suffer do find historical parallels that provide inspiration. African-Americans, for instance, have frequently used the exile and eventual triumph of the Israelites as a central metaphor in their own long struggle on these shores.

New situations keep coming along that remind us of the past.

The arguments about Black promiscuity that were thrown at the civil rights movement of the 1960s (and before) sound stunningly like the arguments used against gay men and lesbians in the 1990s. It's not a new line. In fact, generating images about an "out" group's sexuality is an old method of stirring up the public.

One of the Gentile complaints against Jews in Europe during the nineteenth and early-twentieth century was their alleged "oversexuality." This provided an excuse for pogroms—violent attacks against Jewish ghettoes. Other groups throughout the world, such as the Eta in Japan, have had similar slurs made as they were excluded from the body politic.

The myth of African-American "oversexuality" continues to be used when convenient, pulled out even in presidential campaigns.

When I was a young (white) woman married to an African-American man, more than one European-American and Latina woman said to me with a wink,

"I know why you married him," and made a sexual reference. Strangers said this to me, on the streets of New York, when they saw me pushing my brown babies' stroller and stopped for conversation.

Noticing these historical similarities—as well as the differences—reminds us how often the excuses for bigotry haven't changed. Only the players have.

Publicity about a Black/gay split, which received page one coverage nationally in 1993, is reminiscent of the Black/Jewish split, which first surfaced to media fanfare in 1968. Those two targeted groups had been each other's most frequent allies—and often still are.

The publicity also evokes the recent media focus on Black/Korean conflicts, with the stereotype of Asian-Americans as the "good minority"—a relatively recent image—being used against African-Americans. In both cases, small-store owners restricted by prejudice and tradition from buying elsewhere have caught heat in Latino and Black ghettoes as they absorbed and acted out the wider culture's anti-Black racism. Or, sometimes, simply because they were there.

In each instance antagonisms simmered for years.

And yes, there is long-standing homophobia among Blacks, and widespread racism among gays. There are also sectors of African-American communities that have always been tolerant of a sexual-orientation/ preference difference. Polls on gay civil rights consistently find more support (10 to 20 percent higher) among Blacks than among whites. And there are lesbian groups that have long led the way on anti-racism ally work.

Underneath the friction there are long alliances, however uneasy. We both know what it's like to be permanently marginal; we both know what it is to have nourishing cultures. And, of course, some people are members of both groups—doubly oppressed, doubly blessed.

Competition for scarce seats runs high across the board. Women of all colors, for instance, have found the issue of "race versus sex" frequently used against them when they made demands for sexual equality. The 1991 Clarence Thomas/Anita Hill imbroglio was a case in point. There was one group with real power—represented by those who sat on the Senate Judiciary Committee. Members of two other groups, who didn't have seats, were pitted against each other. There were many plots going on at once, as layers of history overlapped.

As long as we forget that discrimination is discrimination, successive groups will be used to batter each other. One decade many white working and middle-class people believed: All our jobs are being taken by Blacks. The next decade some African-Americans believe that preferential hiring is being widely given to lesbians and gay men, a perception recently voiced to me by a librarian.

One of the arguments now being made against gays—that this is a well-educated, rich, white population with undue influence—was once used, equally erroneously, against Jews. The images persist partly because people with privilege often feel safer to be "out." Thus today wealthy, white gay males are the dominant gay image, a far from accurate one.

In the nineties, as lesbians and gay men begin to gain a smidgen of political power, the fear of getting left behind—again—surfaces. My friend Sam, with a great deal of history on his side, says, "African-Americans started an extraordinary civil rights movement thirty-five years ago, which opened up political and cultural energy the whole country is *still* feeding from. Now everybody is hopping on the diversity bandwagon. It's just like what happened with the blues, with rock and roll, with jazz, with rap. Every time we start something good white folks benefit from it. And we get zip. If they put a gay curriculum in the schools, we won't have Black history anymore. You can count on it."

In order to keep this fear from becoming reality, we all have to see to it that the diversity bandwagon doesn't just briefly raise one group after another to visibility, only to cast them down after their moment in the media sun. We need to find a table big enough for all of us.

As Dr. William Gibson, national NAACP chair, said in response to a question about why the NAACP was a sponsor of the 1993 March for Lesbian, Gay and Bisexual Rights, "I felt it was right for the NAACP to be represented there, because our tradition, objective and constitution is the elimination of segregation and discrimination in all walks of life, for all citizens of this country."

We all need to honor that tradition. It is our national treasure. Every justice movement in the U.S. has as its great taproot the genius and endurance of African-American resistance, with its constancy of struggle and vitality of culture. Let us now praise the generations of African-Americans who created that long resistance, and the little-known women and men—many of them lesbian and gay—from whom we all continue to draw sustenance.

What Is the Place of White Men at the Diversity Table?

With all the talk about the diversity table, what is the coming place for heterosexual white men? Are they going to be the "has beens" of our multicultural future? Are white men becoming diversity dinosaurs?

It's a fear many white men have expressed. "What about me?" is the underlying text in many a complaint of "reverse discrimination," the "tyranny of political correctness," or the "chilling effect of sexual harassment law" on workplace camaraderie.

And what indeed will be the fate of this group, this

25 percent of the U.S. population—heterosexual white males—who currently hold more than 90 percent of the political, economic, and cultural directorship seats?

A power shift is taking place, slow though it may be. The transformation we are experiencing is similar to the power shift currently taking place in South Africa, though on a more subtle level here. Those who have "had it all" may some day have just their fair share—about one quarter of the pie. And that could feel like having nothing at all.

We're in a transition time. Still, men aren't supposed to ask for help, even when they need it, and women aren't supposed to be in positions to extend it. The confusion over men's roles today is evidenced in every arena. For instance: the brouhaha that erupted over the Houston Oilers' response to David Williams missing a game to be with his wife during the birth of their first child. The management's threat to dock pay and suspend Williams brought on major public criticism. As a *New York Times* headline asked, "At Issue: Hold a Baby or Hold That Line?"

Being a man may not be all it's cracked up to be. In addition to facing rapidly changing rules, there's the socialization: being taught not to cry, not to display emotions other than anger or lust for fear of being labeled "sissy."

Men have been so conditioned not to show emotion, even happiness, that they often can't display the warmth they really feel. One of my former clients, a

CEO, is a perfect example. He had a gruff exterior. In fact, he was widely known in his company as a negative, even vulgar, person. After I got to know him well, I discovered that he was a sensitive, deeply caring and understanding man, quite sophisticated, in fact, about gender diversity.

One day I said to him, "Jim, you're really a wonderful person. Why do you have this terrible demeanor?"

His reply stunned me. "If I let it out, they'd eat me alive."

Although the harsh cover may have protected him from a certain kind of attack from other men, it ultimately didn't serve him well as a leader. He was unable to provide the positive vision that people in the organization needed when it was downsizing. His leadership style was just too negative and, eventually, he was forced out of the company.

In addition to the conditioning not to "let it out," many men have the expectation that they will have to learn to kill. In or out of war. In fact, one middle-aged professional man, the son of a Greek immigrant, told me recently that whenever he sees another man coming toward him on the street, he does an automatic assessment of size, wondering "who can take who," accompanied by a flash thought: Kill or be killed.

No wonder men get frustrated when, after all their hard work at self-control, discipline, and numerous other kinds of strengths, they find themselves attacked for not being sensitive, for not 'getting it'!

"I did it right, and now you're switching the rules on me."

In fact, some of that conditioning men get can be useful to keep, and useful for the rest of us to learn. The expectation that one can be tough and powerful—and that this is positive—can be useful to women, who often have an overabundance of nurturant conditioning: Everyone else before me.

Each of us holds a piece of the puzzle, with the different perspectives our varying experiences have given us. That giant puzzle of how to make this planet work needs all of the pieces to be complete.

Heterosexual white men aren't multicultural "has beens." They're becoming "also be's" instead of "only be's." That's not so bad, really. But it's a change, and a challenge, to have mates in power.

Is Coalition Possible?

It isn't always easy working with people from groups with which we are not familiar. In fact, it's often uncomfortable. And old bits of our history get in the way.

There is a lot we don't know about each other. So we often grab at stereotypes. They may provide misinformation, but the human mind needs *some* information to proceed in thinking about these issues. We take in whatever data is floating around—and then wonder why we can't work together to solve our common problems.

For example:

There are real differences: between men and women, between people from different backgrounds, cultures, religions and classes. When we work side by side, I may have trouble understanding your accent or your pace. I don't get your metaphors, your sense of timing. I don't understand your silences or your relationship to your extended family. Your food burns my throat. When you tease me, I am wounded—and years later ask you about it, only to find that it was a form of friendship you were expressing.

You have questions about my choice of a same-sex partner. My optimism. Sometimes even my laugh says "white woman" and you shrink away from me, remembering others who have laughed in the same way and then betrayed you at a crucial moment.

My style of conducting the meeting shouts "woman," and you are impatient. I think you—a male—are impossibly abrupt. I despair at your lack of negotiation skills.

We are both momentarily frozen with discomfort before a woman in a wheelchair. And she herself, a woman of German origin, thinks English-only should be mandated throughout the U.S. She's quite hot about it.

So we come full circle. How can we work together, with all of these differences—some subtle, some glaring—in the way we approach a problem, a life?

Yet how can we not?

Without dialogue, and all the effort it sometimes takes, the isolation continues, and the desperation to make sure "my issue" gets addressed.

The wonder of human beings is our seemingly limitless capacity for growth. We can learn about each other much more quickly than we might have imagined, when we take the time to notice each other. We can make "my" issue and "your" issue and "her" issue *our* issues. In the process we triple our strength.

The People with the B's on Their Foreheads

When I was in my twenties and very angry—about racism and sexism, about Vietnam, about everything—I said to my friend Ann Mari, who was a little older than I, "All of the bad people should just be taken out and shot."

"Oh," she glanced at me with a funny look. "And who are they? The ones with the B's on their foreheads?"

I admired Ann Mari tremendously, so she stopped me in my angry tracks.

It's a question that has remained with me for twenty-five years. Who indeed are the "bad" people who are causing all the pain?

Over the years I have come to understand that none of us has a single social identity. In some parts of our lives we've each had access to that permanent seat at the table. In other parts of our identity we have been (or may be in years to come, as an old person) one of those who is vying for a seat.

We each have our unique diversity profile. My friend Luther, for example, grew up with English as his first language, giving him access to one of the permanent seats. Yet he's Wampanoag—oops, maybe he won't get a seat. Oh, but he's male. And able-bodied. So he's moving back in. But he didn't go to college. Down he goes to the foot of the table. And then there is the matter of age. Twenty-five years ago, when I met him, he was "just right"; now he's "too old" to get one of the better seats.

There are many myths about who we actually are in this country. Often our ethnic backgrounds are hidden, in order to conform to an "Anglo" facade. People who do have English-heritage backgrounds often believe that they aren't "ethnic," they don't have any culture and are simply "regular"! It's true that English heritage has been the dominant one for much of our history. It's still an ethnic heritage—merely less visible because it is everywhere.

And most of us grow up believing that we are middle-class. The myth of the great middle class is one reason we have so many fine distinctions: upper-middle class, lower-upper-middle class, middle-class, on the high end of lower-middle class, lower-middle class, barely lower-middle class, and so on.

We each got messages—often contradictory—early in our lives about where our "place" at the table was to be. Or if we were to have any place at all.

Some of the places, based on the main identities we presented to the world, were more advantageous than others, with better food and better seats. Yet, having to be stuck in any one place has limited those with even the best seats. Such a restricted table is not, eventually, going to provide a well-balanced meal for anyone.

For example, sexism—a dispenser of terrible seats for women—also gives men some ill-fitting seats. It's easy to see how women are harmed: consistently lower pay, violence, and lowered self-esteem, to mention only three. But what about the ways this inequality also limits men?

Right, you women may be thinking, they're crying all the way to the bank. It's true that men continue to make substantially more pay than women in virtually every occupation. This has to change.

Yet it's also true that males, like females, have been restricted to a small range of acceptable human behaviors, unless they are prepared to endure homophobic and other insults. We've all been color-coded at birth: pink or blue (as well as our ethnic code). And human attributes have all been divided in half: This skill is male, that one is female, this aptitude is male, that one female. It's made it tough on all of us to squeeze our personalities in half.

Men, for example, are as burdened by the expectation that they know everything as women are by the training to act empty-headed. It's a ridiculous paradigm for the distribution of knowledge.

Racism? People of color by any social index—income, health care, life expectancy, the daily hassle factor—get lousy seats. Yet "whites," advantaged in so many ways, are losers too, cut off by our own myths from easy closeness with more than 85 percent of the world's population—most of our fellow beings at the planetary table. The isolation is enormous.

European-Americans also pay the social, economic,

and even life-threatening costs of keeping another
group down. As the *New York Times* commented in an
editorial on September 23, 1993, "Americans need to
understand that the lives they value and those they
don't are intimately connected. The murderous ghetto
children we now grow can no longer be held to prey-
ing on their own."

And homophobia? Lesbians, gay men, and bi-
sexuals, excluded from housing and families, often
fired from jobs, aren't even allowed at the table much
of the time. Yet heterosexuals are also bound by this
prejudice, discouraged from getting "too close" to
same-gender friends for fear they'll be considered
gay. Because of this discrimination, many—especially
men—have pulled back from significant friendships,
one of life's most meaningful gifts.

And any of these exclusions mean we all lose out
on a giant talent pool, when we need all the talent we
can get to keep this old planet spinning.

We each have a stake in this change, opening up
access to all the seats. We each have multiple identities, sometimes conditioned to the "one-up" role, sometimes "one-down."

And none of us have B's on our foreheads. If we
have any letters stamped there at all, they probably
read TMB. For "Trying My Best."

Guilty? Not to Worry

One of the difficulties in making diversity work well is the guilt many of us hold, guilt induced when we realize some of the challenges other groups of people face—often at the hands of "our people."

Guilt does strange things to a person. It's like a glue that keeps everything stuck the way it was. When in the grip of it, we cannot act, even though lack of action is what we feel so guilty about!

I can't even clean my closet when it gets so messy that I feel guilty about it. The worse it becomes and the worse I feel about it (and about myself for letting it lapse), the less I feel able to do. I just reach in, grab something to wear, and close the door as fast as I can. Hoping, I guess, that somehow the problem will go away before the next time I have to open it. Finally, driven by desperation, I make a heroic effort and spend a weekend sorting, sneezing, and getting it all cleaned out. Only to have the cycle repeat in six or eight months.

Guilt seems to have a way of making us want to close the door on any situation, rather than face it calmly and decide what part of the problem we can take on today.

An additional problem with guilt is that it often leads to resentment later, in spite of our inaction today.

"Here I've been good enough to go around feeling

wretched about the situation 'your people' are in, and you still don't thank me! Well, I've had enough of being your friend."

And another ex-liberal is born.

Oddly, when we are driven by guilt—about others—we generally put all of our focus back on ourselves.

For example, if I'm spending my energies trying to defend myself, even internally, as a good person who "didn't mean anything by it" when I did something that was perceived as racist, for instance, then all of the attention is being put on me. Which is part of the pattern and the problem: The person with the most social power generally gets most of the attention.

The good news is that we don't need to go around feeling guilty for what has or hasn't been done in the past—even yesterday—for who is helped by that?

Instead of feeling guilty, I could be freeing up some brain cells to notice what has happened, figure out how to repair the situation, and make sure I don't fall unawarely into the same trap next time. For that task, I'm going to need all the brain cells I can get.

So, scratch the guilt. It takes some discipline, but it's worth it.

We are not liable for the past. We simply need to take action in the present.

Does Diversity Mean
We All Go Our Separate Ways?

The specter of "diversity" often raises several fears: If we highlight difference, isn't there a possibility we will come unglued, as Yugoslavia has done? And doesn't having strong group identities contradict our ideal of a world in which all are treated the same, the don't-notice-that-they're-different message we got at an early age?

"Stop staring," we were told as children when we saw someone with an unfamiliar disability.

"Shh, don't ask, it isn't polite," was often our answer when we wondered aloud about some obvious ethnic, cultural, or religious difference.

The reality is that we continued to notice differences, because they were there. We just got more uptight around people who were different in what we considered a significant way. The more of an effort it became to "act natural" when we weren't supposed to notice any difference, the more frozen our behavior became. And, ultimately, it became easier to be with people much like ourselves.

Differences, when they *have* been acknowledged, have often been used as justifications for unequal treatment. They've been brought forward to "prove" superiority. Differences in the context of inequality have been value-laden, with the value tilting toward the group with more social power.

In our reasonable zeal to contradict such a belief system, we've created another untrue paradigm: that everyone is the same. We're not. There is tremendous variety among groups of people. And there is even greater variety among individuals of every social identity group, which is why stereotypes so rarely fit.

In order for us to create equitable situations for all, we need to acknowledge specific differences in cultures and therefore different needs. A meeting scheduled on Friday evenings, for instance, will have different impact on different populations. Religiously observant Jews will either be excluded, since that is Shabbat, or will be compelled to miss weekly services, much as observant Christians would be faced with a difficult choice if an important meeting were scheduled at 11 A.M. on Sunday.

A diverse environment that acknowledges differences—without ranking them—will give us access to the information we tried to get long ago, with our reasonable curiosity, but were "Shhd" from getting. When we eat together we may choose different items from the menu, but we can all be seated at the same table, having fascinating dialogue while we enjoy our meal.

2

The Old Images

As we move into the future, bringing more people to the table, we keep bumping up against the old images.

I checked into a hotel room recently and found "Eurogel" in the shower. It had a blurb about how clean and sophisticated it was, with Europe as the backdrop. I thought about the connotations of everything European as good. What if the liquid soap had been Asia-gel, Latino-gel, or Afro-gel? It conjures up different images, doesn't it?

That stuff slides in every day.

When I call an airline and reserve a seat for myself, I am often asked about "Doctor Lester."

"Will he be traveling alone?"

Even when Dr. Joan Lester goes out into the world in writing, I sometimes have a miraculous sex change. One of my academic articles on the diversity change process has been cited elsewhere as "expert" theory. And the author was transformed into Dr. *John* Lester. *Twice.*

The linkage which already exists in our minds—doctor equals man—often overrides the new information we get. So we simply don't see it. We select data that supports our existing world view. I do it myself. Did I really think that Latina pediatrician was the nurse's aide? Chalk it up to the poor reading material of my childhood (along with everyone else's) and hope that I noticed my thought before I spoke.

When a friend mentions a physician, I realize that I still often assume male, numerous female doctors I know to the contrary. Those early messages seem to have a long shelf life.

And they persist everywhere. Though African-Americans are moving into ever-new job territory, for example, they are twice as likely to get arrested as European-Americans, for any reason. Being a college professor or an accountant makes no difference. And when it comes to drug arrests, or stop-and-searches, African-Americans are apprehended four times as frequently as whites, although drug use among both groups is roughly equal. As a special report in *USA Today* noted on July 23, 1993, "If there's one area where African-Americans are receiving 'preferential treatment,' it's in law enforcement."

The differential treatment is based on an old image, the image of Blacks as criminals. This may be a carryover from slavery times, when a free African-American was viewed as an outlaw. He had stolen himself and might fight to protect the booty—his body.

This image means that if we see a Black man carrying a computer out of an office building, as a friend of mine was, we're likely, as a first thought, to flash, "Thief!" Because of this conditioned response, my friend Jonathan, a university administrator, was detained by campus police for carrying his belongings from his old office to a new one. I've heard dozens of men of color in seminars repeat this story in one guise or another: a psychologist shopping at a mall in Delaware on Saturday, in old jeans, held for hours on "suspicion"; a banker detained on the New Jersey turnpike one evening as he was driving a moving van carrying his own belongings to his new home—held flat on the ground with a cocked gun to his head. And these are the "professional" examples. Imagine taking that element of protection away—for the carpenter, the factory worker, the burger-flipper.

A woman in a diversity seminar told us, tearfully, that she was hesitant to sit in another seat when we were moving around the room, because there was a pocketbook hanging from the back of the chair. She feared being accused of theft if she was anywhere near that pocketbook.

This insult occurs, sooner and often later, too, in the life of every person of color in the U.S. because of a lingering stereotype. The differential treatment extends to all spheres of our lives.

A dark-skinned Latino walks into a mortgage lender, looking for credit. He is at significantly greater risk of being denied mortgage credit than a white person with an identical financial profile.

The image of him in the eyes of the lender, who is usually a white male, may be that he won't be able to qualify anyway, so the lender doesn't take much time to work with him. The mortgage lender may be a nice guy, one who thinks of himself as unbiased, a man who would never utter a racial slur. He is simply unaware of the impact his biased perception has on his behavior. He may have felt he was doing the borrower a favor by not raising any "false hopes." Thus he didn't bother to show the array of mortgage products available, while he wishes there were more "qualified minority" borrowers around.

The cultural images we carry are common to most of us. One of the strangest aspects of stereotypes is that they have the ability to penetrate even those whom they describe. I have noticed that working-class men and women, for example, often say, "I don't really speak well, maybe you won't understand," before they clearly articulate a brilliant thought. Which is not what the culture expects.

As a woman, I carry many of the same images of women that men do. After all, I grew up in the same culture. I may have a slightly different take but, when push comes to shove, we all received the same images and the same expectations. Thus female lawyers and physicians, for instance, have a harder time getting clients—even, sometimes, from other women, who share the cultural images of competency.

I have asked participants in more than a thousand seminars to draw the first image that came to mind when I said, "a white woman doing something"; "an Asian-American man doing something"; "a Black woman doing something"; "a Latino doing something" . . . and on through each ethnic/gender group. The cultural images people drew were stunningly similar across regions, age groups, occupations, and ethnicities.

I found that white women were viewed everywhere primarily as mothers or performing house-maintenance chores. In the minority of images where they worked outside the home for pay, they were usually teachers.

Black and Latina women were also with children (not always their own), were often cleaning (not always their own homes), and frequently were entertainers—singers or dancers. A small minority were educators.

Asian-American women and men were both disproportionately involved with—you guessed it—computers, math, and science. Except for those who had grass hats and stood in rice paddies.

Native American, Black, and Latino men were

primarily drawn as blue-collar workers or manual laborers, as athletes, idlers or dancers. A few were criminals. (When I asked for "African-American" images instead of "Black," both women and men were upgraded in their jobs to include more educators and public speakers. There was a definite intellectual, and sometimes political, image generated by this term.)

Jewish men were financiers, religious scholars or occasionally jewelers. Jewish women, like other women, were often with children.

White men—everywhere and overwhelmingly— had briefcases, sat at big desks, or were otherwise depicted as professional men. Those not portrayed as professionals were blue-collar workers or were enjoying recreational activities. They were virtually never with children, doing indoor household tasks, shopping, dancing, hanging aimlessly about, or engaged in criminal behavior—all activities ascribed to other groups.

These are the stereotypes with which our culture contends. They have an amazing reach. Thus, a white man brought before a judge will have a slight presumption of character and stability—whether or not that is accurate. And the rest of us will, at some level, be presumed to be whatever our dominant cultural image is.

Of course there is a grain of truth in the images, given our different tracking into different occupations and home roles. But, for the most part, they are widely untrue. Even the "positive" stereotypes—those of Asian-Americans as technicians or of white males as professionals—are untrue for most members of those groups.

Yet, even with the pervasiveness of these images, we can learn to see around them. I have observed such change repeatedly. Take, for example, Max, a client whom I came to know well over a period of several years, during which time I met with him monthly for executive consultation. This was a CEO who, at our initial meeting, told me that he didn't give a damn what color people were: purple, green or striped (I don't know what his planet of origin was). If they could do the job, they had one. But there weren't going to be any 'special programs' on his watch. If 'they' wanted to sue, they could.

And they did. Race discrimination, sex discrimination and sexual harassment suits. He got lots of bad press.

Over the next year Max grappled with his initial perception that "people are crying discrimination to get their enemies," or "they're being used by others to get *their* enemies." Because of the terrible press he was getting, Max began to hold open meetings with his employees, asking them to tell him what it was like for them working in his company. Max listened well. And he began to get it. He began to understand how the climate was different for different groups of people in the corporation.

Then during the downsizing trend of the early 1990s, Max's board of directors insisted that he cut expenses drastically. He went to bat for the employees' organizations he had recently funded: for women, gays, and targeted ethnic groups. He argued persuasively that sponsoring retreats and mentoring programs for these groups was essential to remaining competitive. He made a case that this was an investment that would diminish lawsuits, improve morale, raise productivity, and stop the expensive revolving door. He believed it, and he won.

Today, Max is one of the nation's CEOs most committed to diversity programs. He no longer talks about the purple and green people, because he knows "them" now, and they have become "us."

Unlearning the untrue images we have of each other (and ourselves) is a lifelong process, for the old images are pervasive and are continually reinforced, as media studies have repeatedly demonstrated.

I can testify to the persistence of the old images. I've had lots of practice with cultural change—it's my business—yet I notice with shock that I have a moment of wondering how a woman who has gotten a major appointment will know how to supervise four thousand people, and I never wonder this about a man.

I noticed some years ago, with equal amazement, that I was momentarily surprised when friends of color told me they shopped at health-food stores (what stereotype was *that* contradicting?) or when a gay man told me he was marrying—his partner, of course.

I still think these things sometimes (which I call my cartoon-thoughts, for they aren't really "thinking") in spite of a doctorate in multicultural education, decades of leadership on diversity, and a life that has been full of differences.

No matter how much we do, diversity isn't something we "get," and then that's it. Because of the emotional charge that accompanied our introduction to the old images, it's a constant process. We get it as we live and then we forget it sometimes too, when we hear about behaviors that reinforce our former images (and those are surely the ones we remember the most). Or when we observe life through the screen of our stereotypes. So it's a zigzag process.

These images, because they are so often subtle, are one of the main barriers to our getting closer. Yet getting close to people from a formerly little-known group is one of the best ways of learning to see past the stereotypes to the people who are usually much like ourselves—with some interesting new perspectives we may never have considered.

As we make room at the table, we need to bring our own preconceptions to the surface. That way we can make a rational assessment about whether the old data bank is giving us accurate information for our current lives.

Women and Machinery

One of the persistent images is that of women and machinery. We are not supposed to mingle (unless the machine gets something clean). Here's a typical example:

A friend and I went shopping recently for a personal computer, my first. I was surprised at the universe we entered.

Store number one: Charliss and I walked in together. The white salesman we found was so rude, so surprisingly disinterested in us, that Charliss said, "Let's go."

In the car, we were deflated.

"I don't know if it's racism or sexism," I ventured, "or if the guy is just a jerk."

"Hmmm," she said.

Store number two: Three more white guys. They were neither helpful nor hostile. After a few minutes we drifted out. No one made a move to keep us.

Store number three (which we knew had the best price on the new color model): More white men. Our first salesman was unbelievable.

"Is the screen on this model smaller than the previous model?" Charliss asked.

"That's obvious," he smirked.

I don't know which was more remarkable: his open hostility or the fact that he was wrong.

We found another salesman, Bill, who directed all

eye contact and speech to me, the white part of our pair, although Charliss was clearly the expert. (Salespeople often do the same to a male/female pair, speaking only to the male, no matter who asks the question.) I used the countertactic of looking directly at Charliss as Bill spoke, forcing him to do the same.

Finally, we bought what we came for, and took it home. It was a dud, crashing as soon as it was opened.

So Charliss called Bill. She was put on hold for ten minutes. Then he told her he couldn't help her since he "had customers to deal with." He'd call her back. But he didn't take the number.

I left a message for Bill, using my one bit of leverage, my honorary male status: *Doctor* Lester is bringing the defective computer back for immediate exchange.

We returned to the store. After joking, "What did you do to it? Ha ha," Bill said he'd give us a replacement and started to amble about, while the first salesman came over to show us our "mistake."

"Look," I said to Bill, "we run a million-dollar-a-year business. We don't have time for this nonsense. And you wouldn't help Charliss on the phone. This is not acceptable. We *will* have better service if I'm going to buy from you."

He mumbled a weak reply. Then he hopped about, being helpful and courteous.

Before we left, Bill started to pack up the defective computer for return to the factory, and couldn't figure out which way was up. He started to do it one way, looking perplexed.

"It goes the other way," Charliss said. Bill continued trying to jam it in upside down. Charliss repeated, "It goes the other way."

He continued to ignore her. Finally he turned it over. It fit.

"You're right," he said.

"She usually is," I snapped.

"I'll remember that," he said.

Then he was like our puppy dog, trying to be helpful, speeding us along, and carrying the computer to the car.

We talked about it as we drove back to my house.

Charliss said, "It seems like you have to have an attitude when you go in, in order to get any respect."

"Yeah."

The incident started me thinking about Blacks with attitude, about Black rage, and the common store practice of clerks following around people of color as they shop. I thought about how often whites perceive African-Americans as angry even when they're not, and I thought I had never been treated so rudely by so many in a single day.

Well, almost never. The exception is car dealers. Last year I was actually thrown out of a dealership—a lifetime first—when I insisted on knowing the actual selling (not sticker) price of the car before they "did the paperwork."

"I have a family to feed," the manager screamed at me, inches from my face, "and I don't bring my salespeople in here to be abused by people like you." He pointed. "Get out!"

People like me? A middle-aged woman, normally mild-mannered, a woman with money in the bank and checkbook in hand, eager to buy a $20,000 car. Today.

Sounds rough.

Maybe he objected to the fact that my female partner was with me. Or maybe what he didn't like was that I was a woman who had done her homework and wasn't going to be intimidated. Especially after the previous dealer had told me he wouldn't be "jewed down" just because I had a printout of dealer costs. We had a discussion about that phrase. He said he "hadn't meant anything" and then proceeded to tell me how cheap Jews were. So maybe I did enter the second dealership with an attitude.

I approached the third dealership with caution, demanding to speak directly to the manager.

"Look," I said. "I'm ready to buy. This is the car I want, these are the extras I want, and I will pay you $600 above dealer cost, which is X. Don't say anything racist, sexist, or homophobic, and you've got a deal. If you do, I'm out of here."

He handled the sale himself, treated me well (and gingerly), and I bought a different brand of car that day, from a dealer to whom I will be forever loyal.

The plate-glass window of the dealership that threw me out is the only window that has ever talked to me, the only window that called out for several months, as I passed by, "Shatter me." Humiliation does funny things to a person.

More than one woman has told me a similar story. So, shopping isn't all it's cracked up to be. It doesn't always take a woman's mind off her troubles. And "shop 'till you drop" has a different ring to it if you're a woman buying a car or a computer.

Leona, the Wicked (Jewish) Witch

Negative stereotypes of women in business coupled with those of Jews in business—both unflattering images—all came together in the person of Leona Helmsley, the hotel magnate. Not only is Leona Helmsley a wealthy woman, but she is also Jewish.

The association of Jews with money has a long history in our cultural folklore. Shylock is one such folk character. In fact, there were times in medieval and modern Europe when for several hundred years Jews were denied land and access to many professions. They were then channeled into the only careers available, those regarded as "unclean," in which they did the dirty work for others: money lending and tax collecting. And came to be regarded as dirty them-selves. (This is similar to the channeling of African-Americans into sports—through denial of other op-portunities. They then became associated with that one profession, as if it is "natural.")

Thus the history of myth surrounding Jews began, associating them with great wealth and greed. Enter Leona Helmsley. A wealthy Jewish woman, first ac-cused and then convicted of tax fraud. We watched her fall before our eyes. As Leona made her way to prison, news reports recounted her past. She was widely referred to as a woman who "clawed her way to the top."

A man with a similar rags-to-riches story, when found with *his* hand in the cookie jar, is often referred to as "self-made." Never has he had "claws" with which he climbed to the top of the pile.

The venom directed against Leona was unusual. We heard endlessly the details of her arrogant, mean-spirited behavior and "opulent environs." She truly became our Wicked Witch.

There have been many prominent men in the past few years who have been charged with, and some convicted of, various tax-evasion schemes, insider deals, and banking improprieties. Many of them have behaved arrogantly. Many have lived extravagantly, while denying a reasonable livelihood to others.

Yet not a word about claws. There were no widely repeated details of haughty, mean remarks to subordinates. It just doesn't catch our fancy.

So the images live on. Women, and especially Jewish women, were vilified in the person of this one arrogant old woman. It is similar to the Clarence Thomas case, in which a stereotype of African-American males as sexual predators was reinforced, again through the agency of one highly visible, unappealing, token.

Who's Looting Whom?

"Looters." Another image.

It usually refers to people—often people of color, and almost always poor or working-class people—grabbing things from stores. Looting is roundly condemned.

Yet on a grander scale, who is actually looting whom? When people plunder continents and steal the contents—people or minerals or things that grow—they often leave quite a scene of devastation behind. In fact, one of the main reasons for the "advancement" of the West and the "underdevelopment" of the rest of the world is the transfer of resources that has taken place over the past five hundred years.

Sometimes the continent-looters are condemned for it, sometimes honored.

In the words of labor organizer Mother Jones (as paraphrased by Ronnie Gilbert), "When you steal something small, all you get is jail. If you're going to steal, why don't you steal a railroad? Then it'll get named after you, and you'll become a United States senator."

Most people can't get their hands on a continent, or a railroad, when they have looting in mind. Actually, most of us can't even find a good S and L.

Wait a minute, here's a news report. "Angry protesters burned police cars, set firetrucks ablaze, burned down a police station, beat police—seriously injuring some—set parked cars on fire, tore down police barricades, and hurled gasoline bombs, bottles, and metal pipes at soldiers."

Reporting the riots in Los Angeles, right? Or another U.S. city? No. "Pro-democracy demonstrations" in Thailand, 1992.

It's a funny thing. "Riots" erupt in South African townships and in United States ghettoes. When riots continue for more than a day, they are "violent outbreaks" by looters, criminals, or gang members.

In Europe and in parts of Asia, when "pro-democracy demonstrations" continue for a few days and many things are burned, they become uprisings or rebellions. Participants are protesters or, if they die, heroes. And they are ignited to expressions of rage by "dreams of freedom," a noble sentiment rarely ascribed to people of color in the United States today.

The impact of our skewed cultural images of people of color was brought home to me personally by a friend, a woman who is second-generation mainland Puerto Rican. Her son, Armando, went to his high school guidance counselor wanting information about McGill University in Montreal. He had been to Montreal on a school trip and fallen in love with the city. And the university had exactly the courses he was seeking. The guidance counselor, a European-American woman, didn't bother to look up any of Armando's records, but told him that it was an extremely demanding school to which it would probably be futile to apply. She thought he should set his sights on a state school.

Armando came home heartbroken and full of questions about his scholarly ability. He believed, understandably, that the guidance counselor had an accurate grasp of the situation, since that was her job. His parents tried unsuccessfully to restore his self-confidence. And he did go to a state school, close to home.

The story was upsetting to me when I heard about it, as it was to his parents. Yet this one has a happy ending. Through his undergraduate success Armando regained his academic confidence and is about to receive his doctoral degree from a prestigious Ivy League university.

It is tempting to condemn the guidance counselor for being so insensitive. Yet I understand how she overlooked the brilliant scholar in the person of this young Latino. It simply wasn't what she expected. She was acting on the basis of her cultural image, and was too busy to look up Armando's records (if she could remember his name, which many teachers confused with the three other Latino students in the school).

I have caught myself making similar snap judgments. For instance, I was shocked some years ago to hear myself explaining to a new African-American friend I'd invited to dinner what spaghetti squash was. This was a woman who had traveled the globe repeatedly, unlike myself. And this was knowledge I think I would have taken for granted in others and would have never thought of mentioning (even though I was fascinated with the way it uncurled).

Fortunately, she was a compassionate and urbane woman who had undoubtedly encountered similar situations before; she chose to overlook my lapse, if she noticed it, and became a friend.

Age Spots, Wrinkles and Laugh Lines

And then there is age.

"I never minded getting older before," I recently told a friend, with some puzzlement.

"Well," he said, "no wonder. You never were this old before."

As a feminist, it's been hard to admit my feelings about age. I hate to acknowledge that I don't like the lines on my face or the "age spots" on my arms. Or that I notice with discomfort the moments when I don't take gray-haired people as seriously as I do younger ones—but not people who are *too* young.

Ageism is a fascinating "ism" because we move through it so differently than any of the others. We all start on the "down" side as young people, often deeply discounted for our inexperience.

Most of us were eager to get older each year, even counting quarter and half-years: "I'm ten and a half."

"Well, I'm ten and three-quarters, so I'm smarter than you."

We associated aging then with knowledge, power, and privileges.

"When I'm sixteen I can drive." "When I'm eighteen I can drink, or vote, or move out on my own."

Then come the years of young adulthood, though even at thirty jokes start being made, uncomfortably, about being "over the hill."

The ages of twenty-one to forty are considered the "prime years." Those are the years we're on the "up" side of this ism.

If we're lucky, we live long enough to become middle-aged, and shortly, "old." Oops, we're on the "down" side again. And then the idea of aging bringing knowledge, power, and privilege dissipates. Sometimes we feel uncomfortable about naming our ages because we don't want to be discounted as "has beens" by those who are younger.

The reality for me is that I've never been as clear headed, focused, or skilled as I am now at fifty-three. I am in a terrific learning/growth spurt, and having lots of fun at it. When I examine the lives of friends who are my age and older, I observe that the same is true for them.

How strange that the reality is so at odds with the stereotype. But then, isn't that just the way with stereotypes? Some of the people with the most sophisticated linguistic, musical, and spiritual cultures are considered "culturally deprived." And those of us who have acquired wisdom through our journeys of a half century or more are considered "too old to know what's going on."

This is an ism that is creeping up on me, year by year, but I'm going to creep right back at it. And, just when it thinks it's got me—frowning at another wrinkle—I'm going to turn that wrinkle into a smile line and say, "Aha, I've got you, nasty little *ism*. If you ever show your face around here again, you'll be turned into a *wasm*."

Who Is Family?

One of the areas of life where most of us still live inside a stereotype is in our idea of family. The tension between image and reality surfaces in conflicts that are erupting with increasing frequency over child custody. The law—a codification of an earlier image—hasn't caught up with the new reality. Thus the conflict. We see it in "surrogate mother" and some other adoption cases, in which questions of biology, technology, and care-giving all influence our evolving definition of *family*. We see the conflict in child custody cases involving lesbian or gay parents. The law in some states has begun to recognize same-gender couples as co-parents for adoption, custody, and foster-care. Yet most don't, so there are many legal contortions as we try to force a reality without legal standing into an old mold. As more and more "family" arrangements are created and actually lived, written policies are slowly being adjusted to reflect the reality they are regulating.

Less than 7 percent of people today live in the old-model family: two parents in one home, dad works, mom stays home with the kids. (This is the family derived from the Latin *familia*, meaning—literally—a man's possessions: women, children and cattle.) Yet that is still, in some respects, the mental norm for most of us.

"Regular" is how I thought about my family of origin. Daddy worked, mummy was home except when she was at her part-time job, which didn't really seem like a job to us. I expected that when I grew up I would create a family that functioned pretty much the same. Everyone in my original family was all white. (I didn't notice that then. Virtually everyone I knew was white.)

When I did grow up and announce that I was going to marry an African-American man, the reaction I got was my first clue that my life wasn't going to be a rerun of any movie clip I'd ever seen. Most of my original family didn't come to my wedding, my grandparents were furious, and my mother told me that I was going to kill my father with a heart attack. It wasn't at all the way weddings were supposed to be.

That was just the beginning. "First comes love, then comes marriage, here comes Joan with a baby carriage." The years of jumping rope had drummed that into me, and I played it according to plan.

We had children.

But whenever we went out, no one thought we were a family. Once a woman in a grocery store on Martha's Vineyard asked me if my children were from the Fresh Air Fund. People on the streets of New York asked me, "Where did you get those kids?" Everybody was curious, and everyone seemed to feel quite comfortable commenting.

"Your children are so tan." This was said while I sat in the waiting room at the pediatrician's, in a way that demanded an answer. It got annoying to have to create quick comebacks when I was out for simple daily tasks, out for a stroll.

And, as people questioned me, I clung all the more tightly to my children, claiming us as a family. Legally, we weren't even supposed to exist. Culturally, there was a slim space of images in which we lived, and most of them were tragic.

One day when my daughter was a baby, I was arguing (again) with a white taxi driver about race. It was 1966, the height of the civil rights movement. The driver exploded when another driver pulled in front of him.

"They shouldn't let those people drive!" he yelled. "They can't operate machinery!"

Finally, when I demurred on the mechanical skills issue, he brought out his ace:

"You wouldn't want your daughter to marry one."

"She *is* one."

He had a quick case of whiplash trying to see the baby in my lap, and I thought we might not make it.

Only once were we recognized as family. At an amusement park, when my daughter was twelve, the young man taking our tickets for a ride said to us, "You and your daughter can go in now." My head swam with pleasure. We were seen for what we were, a mother and a daughter.

Later on, when my son was home visiting from college, we met in town one day for lunch. It was supreme. We were deep in intimate conversation over our meal, then meandered back toward my car after checking out a few bookstores. On the way to the car, one of us thought of a game we'd often played when he was younger.

"Race you to the car!"

I passed my large handbag to him, thinking to

more equalize the race since he was a twenty-year-old athlete. We raced the few blocks, my heart singing with delight to be talking and playing with my beloved son. As we neared the car, two young white men yelled something at us. I couldn't make it out, and paid it no mind. When we arrived at the car, both of us laughing, they walked by and mumbled "Sorry" as they quickly passed, heads down.

I suddenly understood. They hadn't seen a family. They had seen a young Black man with a pocketbook, fleeing a pursuing middle-aged white woman. My heart trembled as I thought of what could have happened if we'd been running by someone with a gun.

Later, I mentioned the incident in a three-day diversity seminar I was conducting at a Boston corporation. A participant related it that evening to his son, a police officer, and asked the son what he would have done if he'd observed the scene.

The answer: "Shot out his kneecaps."

When the seminar participant told me that the next day I trembled again.

The definition of a family when I was growing up was a mother, a father, and children. So after I got divorced, I tried hard to fill the missing "father" slot. I didn't want us to be a "broken" family.

I tried, but that slot would not be properly filled.

Then, when my children were young teenagers, I met Carole.

Nothing like this had ever happened with anyone

I'd heard of when I was creating my original model of family life. There was no image, or language, to describe all the relationships involved, with each other and with members of each other's biological families. *Partner* sounds businesslike, *mate* is archaic, and *lover* has a fleeting connotation. *In-law* isn't accurate, *out-law* is too flip. But we are all family in our behavior and in our bonds of love, deepening over the decades.

People from cultures other than my own have long had "aunts" and "uncles" considered to be family, although they were not biologically related. I honor those definitions and yet, true to my legalistic culture of origin, have never considered them my own.

However, as I reflect, lots of people didn't consider any of my family such during these past thirty years. So I'm broadening my definition. I've just offered to be godmother to the as-yet-unborn children of my friend Jamie, an African-American gay man. Now he's family too.

Women in Politics: Steel Minds or Empty Heads?

Having a strong woman like Hillary Rodham Clinton in high visibility is a fascinating exercise in observing a string of contradictory stereotypes about women being superimposed upon one person's features.

In 1993 Hillary was widely trashed for wanting to bring the "politics of meaning" to the White House and, indeed, to the folks outside it, too. She was attacked on the premise that articulating moral judgment was a departure from the liberalism of the past thirty years.

In actuality, the entire civil rights movement, and all equity movements that followed it, have been based on a moral premise: If the country really knew what injustices were occurring, people wouldn't allow them to continue. Thus, dramatizations of our various plights, designed to inform and arouse the citizenry.

We were, after all, the children who had grown up in the "land of the free and home of the brave," and were shocked to discover in adolescence that in fact it was the land of the free white man and home of the brave Indian. So we set out to make things right.

The notion that there has not been a level playing field has been the simple underpinning for every equity effort, from the movements for African-American access to women's equality, *La Raza*, disability and gay civil rights.

The attacks on Hillary have not been about her well-defined social goals. They are about a woman unashamed of her power, a woman articulating a clear moral, social, economic, and political vision. Hillary Rodham Clinton is doing exactly what leaders are supposed to do: Give us the view over the mountain so we will know some of tomorrow's possibilities.

But how many women with the national presence to articulate vision and the power to effect change have we ever had in the United States? The image still disturbs many, even in this "era of the woman," and some people will try anything to cut us down to our former size.

First, Hillary was charged with being flip and independent—the "stand by your man" and "cookies" comments—in short, a woman with attitude. When that didn't succeed in derailing her she was vilified for having ambition. Ah, ambition. What woman who has ever held power or aspired to it has not heard this charge? Still, Hillary stood.

Then came "the vision thing." If any of our past six presidents had uttered sentences half as articulate or visions a tenth as broad as Hillary's, he'd be enshrined today as a great thinker, an extraordinary statesman.

We never, any of us, thought it would be this way. We aren't used to seeing anyone other than a (tall) white man be in charge of the really big things. Thus, anyone else is seen as incompetent. Flaws that could be overlooked in commanding (preferably wealthy) white men seem magnified in others.

So, for example, Adam Clayton Powell, a great leader, was kicked out of Congress decades before ethics became fashionable in that body. Shirley Chisolm, a social visionary, was laughed out of presidential politics as "unelectable" before she ever got a good start. Jesse Jackson, surging in the popular vote during the 1988 primary, attracted scathing stories about his ego in major news magazines, thereby providing cover for the inside-the-party ambush.

And now, we have Hillary. One day she was a cold, steel-minded usurper of the presidency. The next day she was an airhead, searching naively for ways to do good. And on day three, when she presented the health care plan to Congress, she ascended. With her "perfect" charm, sincerity, and intellect, she became, as columnist Mary McGrory said, "Eleanor Roosevelt with a law degree."

They are all classic portrayals: the "ball-breaker," then the piece of fluff, and now the Perfect Woman. The latest is far more positive than the others, but what will happen when she errs? Is there room in this image for human failure?

One of the areas where Hillary, surprisingly, had not been condemned when this book went to press was as a mother. Women have long been highly visible and easy targets in this role: too smothering— or too neglectful. Too demanding, too lax.

In 1993 two women lost the chance for appointment as attorney general because of their mothering responsibilities. How telling that the female version of Watergate was Nannygate.

Mother's Day: Hearts, Flowers and International Politics

The epitome of this sacred (though widely trashed) role for women is Mother's Day. Hearts and flowers, cherishing mom, mostly for how well she took care of us. Rarely do we honor our mothers for how well they attended to international affairs. Nor do we usually think of mothers—or grandmothers—in political contexts.

In fact, it is often considered amazing to mention a woman's grandmother status and then tell of an achievement, such as climbing a mountain or winning a congressional run. Never are men described in headlines as "Grandfather Climbs Mountain" or "Grandfather Wins Senate Race." Certainly many men who do these things are grandfathers, but their reproductive function isn't their primary identification, as it still often is for women.

Surprisingly, the origin of Mother's Day in 1870 was as a call to action on international issues.

"Arise, then, women of this day!" the original Mother's Day proclamation began, in the rhetoric of the time. "Say firmly: 'We will not have great questions decided by irrelevant agencies.'" The proclamation was a plea to women to take the major international issues of the day into their own hands and to stop supporting the men who were not able to provide peaceful settlements of those issues.

The proclamation continued: "Our husbands shall not come to us, reeking with carnage, for caresses and applause."

Mother's Day was an appeal for women to "leave all that may be left of home for a great and earnest day of counsel," a day in which women would meet "for a general congress of women without limit of nationality . . . to promote the alliance of nationalities, the amiable settlement of international questions, the great and general interests of peace," wrote Julia Ward Howe.

In other words, women were urged to act publicly, to discuss and influence international issues.

Mother's Day was initiated during the great suffragist movement of the 1850s and 1860s when those women free to do so were leaving home in droves, becoming involved as active citizens in the great issues of the day: the Anti-Slavery and Women's Rights movements. It was a period in which women had found that they could indeed influence events, acting in solidarity with each other in "general congresses." Mother's Day was initiated as a bid to women throughout the world to gather publicly to take action.

And now that day has evolved into one in which women are honored for their private roles within the family—one of the main roles into which all women are typecast.

We've lost this segment of herstory, and thus a piece of our past that would have contradicted some of today's stereotypes of women. This was the segment in which we dared to make proclamations to women of the world, in which we dared to believe that we could effect the "amicable settlement of international questions." Not only is our bold herstory erased, now we have in its stead a day in which women's domestic roles are sanctified. What a diminution of scope.

As we honor mothers next Mother's Day or as we ourselves are honored, let us pause to remember the origins of the day, in which women's sphere was rightly regarded as the world.

Gays, Where Did They Go? (That's Research)

One of the images about lesbians and gays is of sexual predators who are everywhere.

Another image—its flip side—is that we are actually tiny in number.

There are lies, damn lies, and statistics. The "research" that popped up in 1993 on page 1 across the country, indicating that gays hardly exist—1 percent of the population—is all three.

Timing is everything in life, they say. This research appeared at a time when gay people were visible in a way we have never been before, a time when a gay presence in the military, in schools and workplaces, and as parents was being hotly debated. It appeared during a period when the concerns of lesbians and gays in every arena, from housing to health care, were part of an unprecedented national dialogue. In fact, it occurred on the eve of the largest civil rights march in the history of the United States, in April 1993, with almost half of 1 percent of the U.S. population—a million people—in attendance.

As gay power builds, the numbers game has appeared. Each targeted group gets undercounted in its own way. American Indians, Latinos/Latinas and African-Americans, for instance, regularly get creamed in the census, providing a rationale for under-representation at every level.

The question in research always is: Who is doing the counting, and why? What is the trust level? The new numbers for gays (young men only) were based on data compiled from "face-to-face interviews." Respondents were found by cold-calling—knocking on doors. Twenty-five percent of men who answered their doors declined to answer at all. Those who did were asked to supply Social Security numbers, among other identifying data. This at a time when sodomy laws are enforced in many states against gay men.

The interviewers were all female. Were they gay affirmative? We know in social science research that the identity of the interviewer significantly alters responses, as does the language of the questions.

Given the social stigma against "homosexual" sex (and with the question asked this way, as the results were reported, a lack of connection to the gay community was already made evident), given the fact that an interviewee faced potential loss of face, loss of job, even loss of life, why in the world would a man acknowledge—to a stranger—"homosexual" acts?

Millions of people have not acknowledged or are only in the process of acknowledging their gay orientation, choice, or behavior *to themselves*. This acknowledgment is an essential part of the gay experience; it is a lengthy and powerful process, as we gradually become comfortable with this perhaps unexpected, yet central, aspect of our being.

The significance of this process is the reason coming-out stories are ritually told whenever gay people gather for the first time. These stories are part of our celebration, they are descriptions of our courage, they are accounts of how we came over. Coming out is not a one-time event, for we are constantly in new situations in which we must assess safety and quickly calculate acceptable risk. Coming out is not a casual act. Yet this is what the young men in the recent study were being asked to do.

Many men have committed suicide rather than answer questions honestly about their sexual behavior. A client once told me of a suicide attempt after several gay sexual encounters, before he went permanently back into the closet. How might he have answered this question about his past behavior?

This study reminds us that research is always conducted in a social context, released in a social context, and put to some social use. Sometimes that social use is positive. And sometimes it isn't. During segregation, research was used to "prove" that Negroes were intellectually inferior to Caucasians. Lots of data over many years was accumulated about cranial-size measurements. Hard numerical data. Long, learned studies were published and reported—in the *New York Times*, no doubt—demonstrating the inferior mental capacities of Negroes. This was widely believed and described as fact well into my teens. I remember reading all about it in my *Encyclopedia Britannica*.

Research was used to "prove" that would-be immigrants from Southern Europe were mentally inferior to those from Northern Europe—and the first IQ test was developed to screen out just such undesirables.

Research has told us all sorts of things about women of every ethnicity. We've been prone to hysteria because we have wombs, and heavy-duty hormones taken for a few decades won't hurt us. There's probably a soon-to-be-discovered gene for housework, of which guess who will have an abundance?

The latest research on gays is not consistent with data from many other animal species. Nor with the real-life experiences of many of us. For example, Richard, an openly gay Chinese-American lawyer in his thirties, told us in a seminar that he and a few friends had conducted an informal study of his Midwestern high school graduating class of slightly more than four hundred. Examining the men only, they found that about 10 percent were gay, most of whom were not "out."

So, 1 percent? I doubt it.

Yet the headlined reporting—of a small item in a larger study of sexual practices—was instructive as an example of the re-creation of a stereotype which perhaps was losing its grip: the image of gay men as rare, and therefore aberrant.

Passing: Who Isn't?

We, all of us, have developed different ways of coping with the stereotyping of our group and of ourselves. Most of us face some stereotype, whether it's based on our class ("trash" or "snob"), our ethnicity ("drunken Irish"), or some other way in which our group is regarded as inferior.

We all try to live free of the stereotypes attached to us. Sometimes we do that by making ourselves as different as we can from the image. We try not to act "too Italian" or "too Indian," "too Jewish" or "too Asian." Lots of African-Americans, for example, have told me that they were never allowed to eat watermelon as children, because that would reinforce a demeaning image.

Another, more extreme coping strategy has been simply to "pass" into the dominant group, as people frequently do with age and with sexual orientation. Because this happens in lots of situations, intentionally or not, passing is an issue for most targeted groups.

Blacks in the South used to be able to get into "white only" movie theaters by dressing as Africans or by talking with an "African" accent. My ex-husband did this as a young man in Nashville, Tennessee. On Saturday afternoons he and his friends would wrap turbans around their heads, "talk African," and pass on into the theater. What a mix of emotions he must have felt: delight at outsmarting the whites, fury at having to practice the deception in order to see a movie, confusion about why this was necessary.

Looking back through the lens of the current "don't ask, don't tell" military policy, I wonder if the theater personnel were really fooled or if they found the disguise an acceptable way of preserving legal segregation and still getting their revenue?

Passing has been an issue for African-Americans ever since there has been oppression, and the rape of African and then African-American women created children who were sometimes light-skinned enough to pass. Why not pass, and get all the benefits accorded to the dominant group? Why pass, and deny a portion of one's heritage, one's reality? Why live a lie? Tens of thousands of African-American families have been ripped apart over this issue.

Some mostly white families have been torn too. A European-American client, Ethan, described how he felt the need to pass his family off as all-white to his new wife's highly bigoted parents. He removed pictures of his African-American nephew—the son of his sister and her African-American husband—from his home and office, precipitating a wrenching family rift which lasted for years.

Passing. Jews could be in the country club, or the neighborhood, or star in movies, if they just changed their names and, in some instances, their noses. In my uncle's case, the name change was from Steinau to Walker. In my friend Loel's case, his parents made the name change during his childhood from Greenberg to Greene.

Gays can officially be in the Catholic Church if they don't "practice" their gayness. (Is the fear that practice will make perfect?)   Lesbians and gays can often remain in the family if they don't say that their "roommate" of twenty years is their life partner. Everyone knows, no one acknowledges. That's the unspoken agreement.

There have been passing women too: Women have sometimes passed as men to get a job, to be Pope, to walk a street in safety, to roam the world and have adventures. Or to live with a female lover.

So long as there are two classes of people—those with significantly greater and lesser social power— some members of the latter group will try to pass, unobserved, into the former. Why not? Yet at such a cost to self.

So long as the split exists, the edges will continually need to be defined. For who is in, who is out?

Some people in targeted groups choose to pass. They may consider it a matter of survival. For others, passing comes naturally because they don't fit the stereotype. Thus, they are often invisible and, if they wish to be fully seen, need to "come out" about their heritage, sexual orientation, or age every time they meet a new person. This is a common experience for light-skinned Latinos/Latinas and Blacks and for the millions of people with many sorts of mixed heritage.

Who is Black? Are my children Black, with one European-American parent and one African-American parent (who himself has African, Cherokee, and German ancestors)? In the United States anyone with any acknowledged African ancestry is generally considered Black. And the infamous "one-thirty second"statutes supported that. (The first census in the United States listed three categories of "race": white, slave, and other.)

And who is "white"? A fiction created during slavery times to distinguish "us" from "them." Most European-Americans have been considered "white" except Southern Europeans. Carlos, a friend of mine from Spain, married Mercedes, a Puerto Rican woman, and thus became "Hispanic" rather than "European."

Latinos/Latinas have long presented a problem for neat racial classifications. Often they are "white"— or Black—until they open their mouths to speak. Then their language puts them into a different classification. Their mere existence defies racial categories.

Afro-Caribbeans may identify as Latino yet be considered Black in this country. There are huge variations in the racial/ethnic histories of Latinos/Latinas depending on their country of origin, as well as their own family background.

A seminar participant told us this story: His father, Miguel Rodriguez, had come from Spain as a young man. He moved to California where he wanted to marry his sweetheart, an Irish-American woman, whose mother refused consent.

"People will think you are Mexican. Unless you change your name you cannot marry my daughter."

So Miguel Rodriguez changed his name to Michael Ryan, selecting the name of the Irish bishop in his adopted hometown. He didn't tell his children this story until they were in high school. The children had been told by their Irish-American grandmother that their other grandparents, who spoke only Spanish, were "Black Irish."

The same week I heard this story, another man I have known for years, whom I have always considered a British sort of fellow with a British sort of name—John Pembroke—told me that his mother is Puerto Rican, he lived in Puerto Rico as a child with his grandparents, and once he grew up he deliberately passed as Anglo. Only now, as a man of sixty, has he decided to relearn Spanish and reconnect with his island relatives.

Passing. Asian-Americans have variously been considered "white," "Asian," and "other," depending on the political vagaries of the moment. In Boston in the 1960s, the School Board changed Asian-Americans back and forth from "white" to "people of color" several times within a year, as the need for various numbers shifted.

Passing. Who is Jewish? Is a Unitarian who knows Yiddish a Jew? Jewish law says anyone whose mother is Jewish is a Jew. Nazi Germany's definition was similar to that of U.S. Blacks: anyone with any traceable Jewish ancestry is Jewish. You could convert to become a Jew, but you couldn't convert out.

And who is gay? A person who reads a gay magazine? A person who has one same-sex encounter? Six? Ten? What about an affair?

"Don't ask, don't tell" is just the latest version of passing. It is a bitter pill which will continue to be litigated and otherwise contested as military policy, because passing is such a painful experience. And because being lesbian or gay is defined by much more than moments in bed, as is being heterosexual.

Being heterosexual involves particular rituals, like weddings, certain social events in mixed-gender couples, and having a heterosexual outlook on life, in which boy inevitably meets girl.

Being gay involves other rituals, like telling coming out stories and having a different perspective on sex roles, on family, on politics. Being "in the life" is an attitude as well as a behavior. That's why gays and lesbians are so often visible. It's something wonderful and self-confident in the walk of a woman, something sweet in the look of a man. These attitudes are not easily hidden. Yet people try to.

Many people in the United States are passing, consciously or inadvertently, regarding their class, ethnicity, or some other aspect of themselves. There are many communities in hiding, driven underground by shame and fear.

Part of the process of creating a diverse present is the reclaiming of ourselves—the Native American great-grandmother, the Jewish cousins and African-American nephew, the lesbian "maiden" aunts—acknowledging who we really are in all of our multilayered complexities.

3

Now What Do I Say?

As we take our seats at the table with so many others who didn't used to be there, we need a new language. The old language—with its prevalent male pronouns, its color coding of light and dark for good and evil, its virtual absence of language for gays, lesbians and people with disabilities—this language doesn't describe the reality that is emerging.

Newscasters, for instance, fumble and grope for the right phrases when discussing gay "life-styles." Other people have lives; gays and lesbians have "styles." We all wonder what words to use in a variety of situations. When we aren't sure, we often don't say anything. Which leads to further exclusion and invisibility.

Part of constructing this new universe of inclusion, making room at the table, is creating a new language that can describe it.

What's in a Word?

Usually words slide in without our ever noticing, and before you know it, we've constructed a universe.

The media tell us about "tribal" warfare in South Africa, and "black on black" violence there. That's what's happening. And a lifetime of imagery is evoked.

This image was given new life in 1993 during the fighting in Somalia with headlines about Somalian "warlords."

Warlords? This is a term reserved exclusively for Asians and Africans abroad, and African-American or Latino gang leaders at home. Europeans in a similar feudal spot were "lords of the manor"—or, if they were especially warlike, "knights." And who among us, after all, would care to defend the rights of an errant warlord?

Eastern European warfare is called an "ethnic clash." We never hear about "white on white" violence. It's just people from "ethnic" groups clashing. How much more understandable than those enigmatic "tribal bloodbaths."

We also continue to color-code as powerful symbolism for good and evil. The man with the dark hat, riding on the dark horse, is reliably the bad guy. We can still expect the hero to be dressed in white. A white lie isn't a very bad one, a dark and shady character isn't a very good one; fair-skinned means light *and* beautiful, and so on through blackmail, black witches, and dark days—all of them bad.

We're hard put to find positive usage of darkness. I always have a moment of confusion when I hear a business is in the black, having to override my culture and remember that's good. (Yes, there once were red and black pens for the books.) I am struck by the powerful—and in our culture, unusual—image of the fertile dark, germinating seeds and nurturing ideas.

This color coding is so pervasive it begins to feel natural. Yet not every culture shares this color scheme. In some Asian cultures and several U.S. subcultures, funeral mourners dress in white—the color of ghosts, of death.

There is also a gender-based language which we, as a culture, started to notice two decades ago. I remember men walking away from me at parties, furious when I quarreled with *man* and *his* as mislabeling of generic human terms.

It's still a hot topic.

Some people insist that *mankind* means everybody.

"It's just a word," they say.

"Okay then, let's use *womankind* for a few thousand years. Equal time. *Womankind* includes everyone, men and women. We'll study the History of Woman: Paleolithic Woman, Neolithic Woman, Cave Woman, right on up through Renaissance Woman to Modern Woman and her technological revolution. *Woman* is just a word designating everyone when used in this context."

"Hmm . . . it does make you stop and think. But let's not get all hung up on words."

"I won't if you won't. We'll reverse some gender-specific titles, too. We'll have *Chairwoman* and *Woman of the Year*—both of these include men of course."

"Hmm. . . ."

A word is just a word. Yet every word has a past, and not all of them are honorable.

Rule of thumb derives from an English law stating that a man could not beat a woman with any stick wider than his thumb.

Handicap has, as one of its origins, the begging image of "cap in hand." People with disabilities in eighteenth-century England were not admitted to poorhouses, but were sent off with caps, with which they were expected to beg.

"It's only a word," you may be thinking. "Because I say I was 'gypped' doesn't mean I'm going to oppress Gypsies, if I could find any. And when I say he 'jewed me down' I don't necessarily mean anything about Jews."

Maybe not.

And then, if we reverse these terms to speak of tribal warfare in Yugoslavia where there is white-on-white violence of the evilest, whitest kind, where people must be wary in stores of being "angloed" lest they be "christianed" down, it does make a woman think.

Language can be so subtle. A little word like *the* can

make a big difference. The homeless. The disabled. The slaves. The Japanese. The poor, the rich. Faceless groups, defined by one aspect.

How different from: People who are homeless. People who are disabled. People who are, or were, enslaved. The emphasis here is on the persons, who have an isolated, perhaps temporary, condition of their lives being noticed.

For years, when President Bush mentioned them at all, he said "the Palestinians." A few weeks before the Israeli-Palestinian peace talks in Madrid he began to say "the Palestinian people." The phrase evoked an image of a group demanding respect, indicating the U.S. shift toward that conflict.

My friend Barbara tells a story about the power of a word. When Barbara, who is African-American, was living in Tennessee, she took sailing lessons. One day she was in a boat with three European-American men.

"Too bad about the park," they said to her. "It used to be a nice place. Now people don't go there anymore." Barbara wondered what they meant. She had just been to the park. It was full of people. Black people.

A more chilling example of the same phenomenon occurred during the furor over a series of murders of European tourists in Florida in late 1993. The recent murders of local Black residents—one of them in Jefferson County—received little investigative, and almost no journalistic, attention. Bad enough. Then the Jefferson County sheriff told reporters that the murdered tourist slain in his county was *the first person* slain in the county that year.

When white people say "people," the meaning is often white people. The ethnic descriptor is usually used when a person of color is designated—whether or not that descriptor is relevant to the meaning.

Similarly, many of us use *lawyer* (meaning male) and *lady lawyer, doctor* (male) and *woman doctor*, or *classical music* (European) and *Black classical music*. Without the adjective, we assume the maleness or the European origin as the norm.

Unspoken norms convey worlds of meaning. For instance, *the Near East*. Near to what? Europe is the unspoken point of reference. The Far East, the Middle East. Does the whole world use these phrases and thereby have Europe as the geographical center of its mind-set?

Our point of reference sometimes makes all the difference in meaning. Columbus discovered America, or a group of native people found a lost sailor? Polygamy means one man has many wives, or a group of women share one husband?

As Les McCann entitled a tune some years ago, *Real Compared to What?* It's helpful to notice what our points of reference are, so we can consciously choose the images, phrases, and words, and thereby the meanings, that we wish to convey. As well as the ones we are absorbing.

Noticing what language is used all around us, and what language we use ourselves, is a major step toward becoming more inclusive. As we become more inclusive in our words, we usually find our thinking and then our actions reflect the shift. Because we have to think about what we are saying.

At first the changes feel awkward on our tongues. I remember the shift from *mailman* to *letter carrier*, *fireman* to *firefighter*, *girl* to *woman* and *stewardess* to *flight attendant*. It was strange to change a term I'd used all my life. Yet within a year I hardly noticed.

Some possibilities: Sitting Indian-style can be sitting cross-legged. Blackmail is extortion, a black day is a hard one, a master copy is an original, and a rule of thumb can be a guideline.

A word is a small thing. But it can make a world of difference to the listener.

Most of us have "trigger words," words that set us off, making us want to fight or flee. For some it is profanity. A simple word can make us want to kill. For others, it may be a word that has been associated with repression and prejudice against our group.

A woman who was a farmer once told me her trigger word was *farmer's wife* because it made her, as a farmer herself, invisible. So she took to referring to her husband as a *farmer's husband* to make her point.

For many gays, a trigger word has long been *flaunting*, as in "I don't mind gay people as long so they don't flaunt their life-style." A well-meaning ally may say this, having no idea of the hurt and history carried by this phrase. Many lesbians and gay men hear this as: Stay in your closet. Pass. And so long as you're invisible, I'll accept you.

The result is lesbians and gays feeling twice as separated from heterosexuals, many of whom have little awareness of the way they "flaunt" their lifestyle every time they mention a spouse or hold hands or kiss in public, on TV, and in the movies or magazines.

The group with the most social power usually doesn't notice its own language; it doesn't have to. So it can feel uncomfortable to suddenly become self-aware. Thus the common complaint, "I can't say anything anymore. I have to walk on eggshells. How can I have friendships if I can't say what's on my mind?"

The "free speech" we may remember wasn't actually there for everyone in the past. The excluded group long felt silenced and invisible. The discomfort some of us now feel is part of this transitional time when, together, we are figuring out the new language.

What's in a Name?

The group with most social power generally also has the ability to name things and people. So part of the movement toward self-pride and empowerment of an excluded group is to begin to name itself: women, not girls; Asian-American, not Oriental.

Because this naming signifies a greater power struggle, it is often highly charged.

Fifteen years ago I heard a popular talk-show host give a speech to a large auditorium full of people. At one point during his talk he mentioned girls, meaning women.

"Women," someone yelled out.

"I'm used to saying girls. The name doesn't really matter," he laughed and went on.

It mattered to many women there, who began to shout, "Women!"

There was tremendous force behind the shouting. This really mattered.

African-American women and men have battled the demeaning labels *girl* and *boy* for several hundred years.

To an outsider, the discussion about a group name can be confusing, especially because it seems to change rapidly and we don't know why.

"Colored, Negro, Black, Afro-American, African-American, Third World people, First World people, people of color. How am I supposed to keep up? And why bother?"

We can keep up by noticing what terms are being used most frequently by people and media we respect, by asking about it, and by following the discussion. There is always a public discussion about a peoples' changing self-perception. The new name simply reflects that.

And if we plan to succeed in diverse settings we need to keep up, to give respect to others, calling them by the name they prefer.

It may be that an older name becomes somewhat contaminated by oppressive conditions. A new name can enter the scene untarnished, signifying a new generation's hope for a brighter group future. As such it deserves to be respected.

The changing context often means that there is some generational tension as the language is changing. An older generation that fought hard to maintain dignity in the face of words hurled as epithets—*queer* or *black*, for instance—sometimes has difficulty proudly claiming such a word. For a while we may inwardly cringe, even as we applaud the boldness of our younger peers.

"Hispanic, Latino/Latina, Latino-Chicano/ Chicana, Chicano/Chicana, Mexican-American?"

A woman in a seminar said that her grandmother told her when she was young that *Spanish* used to be the prized term for *Latinos/Latinas*. It was good because it highlighted the European heritage while not acknowledging the other heritages. Now that there is more pride in the multiple heritage of Latin cultures— the native Indian and African heritages as well as the Spanish—the name *Latino/Latina* is often preferred, which includes, for some, all of those historic cultures. U.S. *Latinos/Latinas* frequently use that term. Yet for *Latinos/Latinas* in their country of origin, or for those who are first generation, specificity of country—like Mexico, Brazil, or El Salvador—is crucial. That is their identity. So the term *Latino/Latina* is very much a U.S. term, implying a commonality of culture.

Every ethnic group has its own dilemmas. For example: "You say Asian when you mean Asian-American. I'm not Asian, my people have been here for three generations. You have no idea how many times people come up to me and ask me where I'm from, and the look I get when I say, Ohio. When you say Asian to mean Asian-American, you reinforce the stereotype of Asian-Americans as 'foreigners.'"

Then again, someone might comment: "Asian-American? Which Asian-American? A Korean-American, a Chinese-American, a Filipina-American, a Japanese-American? Or an ethnic Chinese person from Malaysia? Who are you talking about? We are all so different from each other, as different as a German is from an Italian, or a Nigerian from a South African, and you lump us all together. Or are you talking about Pacific Islanders, rather than Asians?"

Some people still use the term *Oriental*. For many, there's an air of exoticism attached to that word. It was created by Europeans who "discovered" the "Orient," which they named as such, in contrast to their half of the globe that they named the "Occident." It carries a history of mystery and foreignness.

Another group: "White people named us Indians. We have our own tribal names. We're not one nation.

We were Indians, now there are regional differentiations. In Minneapolis many of us decided a few decades ago to call ourselves Native Americans. Now some of us have shifted back, reclaiming the word that was given to us by Europeans, *American Indians*."

People of color, comprising at least 85 percent of the world's population (depending on how one counts "races"), have all been grouped together in the United States under many labels.

The term *non-whites*, favored by the government for years, has been widely rejected. Why define anyone by what they are not? I wouldn't want to be described as a non-male.

Third World was popular for a while, created by nonaligned African and Asian nations. One problem with this term was that people of color who lived in the "First World"—Europe and the U.S.—didn't always feel included. Others objected to being categorized as belonging to a different "world," which sounded like a different planet. Still others objected to being "third." Some people from Africa, Asia, and South America adopted *First World* to signify their centrality.

People of color is a phrase currently in wide use, although many people object to the invisibility of their own cultural heritage which results from this coalescing of all the world's people except those of European heritage. This term also has the problem of being color-based, and it is not always clear who is included. Is a "white" Latina, one who could "pass," a "woman of color"?

There will probably never be one term that makes total sense, because we are trying to find one term to describe categories—race, color, ethnicity, and culture—that are more fluid and complex than any one word can connote. Furthermore, everyone in a targeted group doesn't get together on one day in a meeting to decide what to call their group, so there is never complete unanimity.

Nonetheless, names do shift, regionally and nationally, and there is significance in the shifts. We begin to talk differently, and as we use the new language we think about ourselves, and each other, differently.

Taking away individual and group names has traditionally been one form of taking power from people. Self-naming is a reclamation of power, thus significant and often contested terrain.

People in the dominant culture often don't understand the emotional charge associated with names. They have the luxury of not having to care because their culture is all around them, and their group has, in essence, named everything and everyone, from "Indians" to "Orientals." Taking control of its name is one form of an excluded group's attempt to assert control over its destiny.

Our Own Names

The flap over Hillary Rodham Clinton's name got me to thinking of my own.

I got my last name of origin, Steinau, from my dad, who got it from his dad who got it from his dad, in a row of Steinaus stretching back to Abraham Steinau in Steinau, Germany. My dad's brother changed his last name as soon as he left home to an Anglo-sounding one, Walker. He even gave himself a II at the end of the name. And with the name came a background. He was from wealthy Southern roots. Not the locked-out-of-the-rooming-house family, with a Jewish bookie father, Jacob, whom my father remembers back in Louisville.

Losing Jewish names is not uncommon. A friend of mine's father changed the family name from Greenberg to Greene when he was very young, a change resisted only by the daughter, then sixteen, who has retained the old name these thirty years. My friend is now considering making the move back to Greenberg.

A number of my friends have renamed themselves as adults: Emma Missouri, Heru Nefara Amen, Aquila Ayana, the Rev. Muate Rasuli, Alake. They have used the name change to claim heritages made invisible by the "forgetting" of our labor her/history or the wholesale erasure of names in slavery times.

Of course, most of our mothers' names get erased all the time. My own mother's name of origin, Barbara

Hill, appears nowhere in my name, nor does she anywhere carry her mother's name, Zilpha Robbins. As remedy to this invisibility, some women have taken names from the maternal line and inserted them into their own: Carole *Lannigan* Johnson, Sally Mariechild, Laura Almajones.

My own last name—my Anglo one—I got from my first ex-husband, who got it from his father who got it from his father who got it from a slave owner. I decided to keep the name even after the man, because of the children, so we would all have the same last name. And I'd gotten used to the name myself.

Then I married another man who didn't like my having the first man's name, but I kept it anyway. Well, I tried to keep it. But the Motor Vehicle Department in New York wouldn't let me get a driver's license in that name because now I was married to another man, and a married woman in New York in 1972 had to use her current husband's last name. So I was going by several names then, with the driver's license in one name and the checking account in another. It made cashing checks difficult, but always an opportunity for education.

Many people's names have been changed by others. Some were shortened and Anglicized by officials with papers at Ellis or Angel Island, or by an employer impatient with foreign-sounding names.

A few years ago Janie worked in my office. One day I asked her about her experiences in London, where she had lived and worked as a nurse and a secretary for ten years after emigrating from Malaysia.

In the telling of her adventures as a woman leaving her native land at twenty, she included, "My employer in London couldn't remember Mei-Ying, so she said, 'We'll call you Janie.' We all got used to it, and that's how I became Janie. Even my husband Kok-wah calls me Janie."

I was appalled. "That's like a slave name. Don't you want your own name back?"

After first demurring, laughing and saying, "Oh no, we are all used to it now," it turned out she would prefer it. In fact, when she said her own name she lit up in a way I had never seen. We all made the switch at the office: Janie quickly faded away as Mei-Ying came forward. And quite a different person she was: not the shy, self-effacing Janie we had come to know, but a dynamic and powerful woman who took leadership at work and then became the first female board member of her church.

Mei-Ying, I salute the woman you reclaimed. *Mazeltov!*

Let us all reclaim our power to name. As we create our language we create ourselves. Let us create ourselves in the most beautiful images we can imagine.

4

Now What Do I Do?

Doing the Right Thing

How can we know what is "the right thing" to do, given the varieties of cultures that we'll never know all about? Well, we may not have it all down perfectly, but we do have one great source of information: ourselves.

Every one of us has been a target for unfair treatment at some time in our lives, based on being "one down." We know what it's like to belong, however briefly, to the group with less power to define and control our world.

There are differences in the impact we received. One may have been thrown against the hood of a police car, wondering if each second was his last, while another was shaken after hearing "chink," "slut," or "dyke" yelled from a passing car. Another recalls being unable to marry the love of his life because he was Jewish, Navajo, or Shoshone. Someone else remembers being hit as a child, as a woman, or because she is old. There is a spectrum in how life-threatening these experiences were.

Yet there are striking similarities in response: feeling like an outsider, with mixtures of shame and rage; doubt about whether this is really happening; moments of feeling helpless, hopeless, or confused about what course of action to take; and wanting to flee, to hide.

These are what we have often seen modeled around us. We do, of course, have a choice about our reactions. And part of our struggle, in those aspects of ourselves that get targeted, is to choose responses that will lead to the most powerful and positive outcomes.

All of us know about the other role, too. We have all, willfully or unintentionally, targeted others at various times.

I recall laughing at the new girl in my sixth-grade class who had cerebral palsy. I remember now with horror how I joined right in with my classmates, imitating her shaking, and can only explain my behavior by also remembering those were the years when I was desperately trying to fit in and to be liked myself. I didn't want to be excluded as she was—so I thought I had to be one of the tormentors.

I have heard thousands of stories in seminars of people being targeted, and stories by people who did the targeting—usually unawarely. I have heard about people of color and Jews being taunted on their way home from school, and heard from the taunters, who, like myself, were only trying to be one of the gang and didn't really think about the impact of their behaviors.

I have heard from women and people of color who have had terrifying experiences of harassment, leading to ulcers, nervous breakdowns, and job losses. And I have heard from men of all ethnicities and white women, some bitter memories of being given little assistance as their workplaces integrated, stories of behaving exactly the way others behaved and then being singled out for accusations of insensitivity or worse. They didn't understand what had hit them, when they were just going along the same as always. They felt betrayed. The rules had changed mid-game, and no one had bothered to explain.

These experiences leave a tremendous emotional charge. No wonder passions run high when we talk about diversity issues as they surface in our daily lives. We have quite a legacy.

All of us are carrying bits and pieces of partially remembered experiences.

An odd little piece that I carry has to do with class. Food was not always abundant at dinner in my childhood home. The small meatloaf—a pound of hamburger "helped" by what I angrily regarded as sawdust--was cut evenly into five portions, served around, and there were rarely seconds. On other nights the can of Spam was likewise sliced, fried, and split into five servings. And the brick of ice cream, or the quart of milk—cut with powdered, which I hated—were evenly apportioned. I often wanted more, and it wasn't there.

To this day it is hard for me to share food. When we have company for dinner and my partner generously offers leftovers to take home, I look longingly at the food as it goes out the front door. She has learned to check with me in advance if she wants to make such an offer.

We each carry these bits and pieces of experience from being "one down." They sometimes surface in the most unexpected places.

One of the wonderful parts of all this is that, at various moments in our lives, we've also had allies— people who were our champions. People who reminded us that there was a world with friends out there.

Being an Ally: To Others

I had a remarkable experience once of having an ally. It occurred many years ago when my partner and I bought a two-family house with friends, a heterosexual couple and their infant son. The house was in a rural area. I was nervous about moving in because there had been several violent attacks against lesbians in that region shortly before, including a burning mattress being placed against the door of a lesbian's house at night. I didn't know of any other lesbians living in the immediate area where we had found our dream house: a fully renovated sixteen-room colonial farmhouse, with six fireplaces, already divided into two living units.

When I told our house-partners how terrified I was, shortly before we moved in, Amy said, "I would never let anyone harm you. I would put my body in front of you, and always stay between you and anyone who was trying to get you."

Because I was so afraid of physical harm, Amy's reassurance of her physical presence was extremely moving. Her words created a vivid image of security in my mind.

Her partner, Tom, was helpful in a different way. He said, "The neighborhood is lucky to have you in it, and everyone will love you. You'll see. Everywhere you go, people love you." Tom held out such a positive image that he convinced me of our welcome—which came to pass. Shortly after moving in, our two households held a lawn party to which we invited all the neighbors. Some of them brought home-baked cookies, everyone had a lovely time, and we spent six happy years living in that house.

My friends' two different kinds of support helped give me the confidence to create the connections with neighbors that would sustain me in the unlikely event we were attacked. They assisted me over my fear and enabled me to be my natural gregarious self. In some ways it was helpful that they weren't lesbian or gay, because they were enough outside the situation that they didn't get terrified themselves. Sometimes people in our own group are triggered by their own fears and memories and they start telling horror stories about the terrible things that happened to them in a similar spot, just when we need to hear something more upbeat. (On the other hand, there are moments when it's totally comforting to be with someone who has shared exactly the same kind of rough time and lived to tell, and perhaps even laugh, about it.)

Being an ally takes lots of forms. It may be simply *not* laughing at a derogatory joke. Or calling harassment when we see it. We are allies whenever we intervene, however subtly, using whatever power we have to move the situation forward.

A young white man who works at an insurance company told us in a seminar how he had become friends with a colleague, a Japanese-American man, and learned how the information loop never reached him. As a result, Al became a vigorous supporter of including Asian-Americans in "minority" mentoring programs. He didn't have a lot of power himself, but he did raise the issue, something his friend was reluctant to do for fear of further isolation.

Another example: Sarah, a Gentile, works as an administrator at a national health organization. She regularly reminds people at her staff meetings not to schedule programs at times that will present a conflict for observant Jews—one of the main ways Jews are made invisible by the larger culture. Sarah bought books for the office about Jewish holidays and had a calendar made for everyone which includes the major holidays for several years, so people can plan around them.

Acting as an ally is a tricky business. There is a fine line between being an effective ally and taking over someone else's struggle. As whites, or able-bodied people, or members of some other group that has frequently been in charge, we are so used to running the show that we often believe we can do it better than anyone else. After all, "cream rises to the top," as a man told me recently on a radio call-in program, explaining why white men have the country's key jobs.

Yes, we've had lots of practice running the show. So it feels natural to take the gavel, literally or metaphorically. The challenge is to know how much to sit back and watch unfamiliar kinds of structures emerge, and when to introduce our own.

It's a delicate balancing act.

Sometimes we want to leap into action. And when we are members of an in-charge group, we do have a great power to intervene in the actions of other people in our group. It is a different strength from those who have been directly targeted. For example, whites will sometimes be listened to by other whites on the topic of racism when a person of color couldn't be heard. (And there are occasions when the opposite is true, as Carol Mosely Braun is demonstrating so powerfully in the Senate.)

A heterosexual who publicly supports expanded partner health benefits may be greeted with less skepticism than a lesbian speaking on her own behalf. And a man speaking up about sexism is very powerful, in certain contexts. Others can't as easily rationalize away his points with an explanation of "over-sensitivity" or "requests for special treatment." We've all learned to give credibility to the statements of that in-charge group.

Sometimes we want to charge right in, as allies, and sometimes we shrink back. "Now I'll be shunned as one of them" is a common fear.

On issues of race, we white people may fear criticism by other whites for breaking rank. The form can range from ridicule to violence. We may be accused of being "idealistic" or "out of touch," discounted much as the target group is.

Many men have told me of their difficulty when among a group of men who are disparaging women. They are uncomfortable with the conversation but have a terrible fear that the taunts could turn toward them.

Homophobia can be a difficult topic for allies because by speaking out, they fear questions will be raised about their own sexuality. I remember teaching a college class years ago and wanting to assign a book with a gay theme and, at the same time, wanting to make sure the students knew I was an ally, not a lesbian. It was so terrifying to introduce the book that all I can remember now is the fear—not even what the book was or anything else about it.

Allies also often fear "doing it wrong." We may be prepared to act, but confused about what to do. What if someone from the group we think is being mistreated is there, and they're not saying anything? Can we?

In fact, most people find that they don't have to have the perfect answer in order to make an impact. Simply breaking the silence, even awkwardly, is powerful, and usually a relief to others, too.

One thing I've learned is to say that something bothers me, rather than, "That is offensive to _____ [naming some others]." Then the person to whom I am speaking cannot pull out their "others," getting us into an argument about whether people with disabilities, for example, "say such things themselves." Or what "they" would think of all this.

I learned this the same way most of us learn things: the hard way.

I had occasion to put this skill to work several years ago when, still living in the East, I stayed at a charming bed and breakfast for a few days while in San Francisco on business. On my last day there, the owner made a disparaging remark about one of the other guests, saying she was squirreling away food from a wedding party being held there. "She's Jewish, you know" he confided, "Jews always hoard." And he laughed.

It took me a moment to gather my wits. Oh dear. It was so tempting to let it pass. Who, after all, overheard us? Would it matter if I didn't say anything? I decided to speak because I knew the remark would rankle me for the rest of the day, or the year. Confronting him would give me closure. And, if he got a little education, so much the better.

"Why do you say that about Jews?" I asked. "I don't think that's true."

"Oh," the man was truly apologetic. "Are you Jewish? I didn't know. I'm so sorry."

"No, I'm not," I said (deciding not to go into that erased Jewish grandfather, and my confusion about how to claim him). "That's not it." I paused. "It just made me uncomfortable to hear you talking that way. That's a reputation Jews have that's not true."

I wanted to stick to my point about the stereotype not being true without necessarily going into thousands of years of Jewish history. If he asked me why I thought it wasn't true I'd go into it, otherwise I simply wanted to let this man know that what he said wasn't okay with me. And perhaps he would think a little more next time before he made a similar remark to a guest.

"I didn't mean anything by it," he tried to retract.

"Okay." I said. "It just made me uncomfortable. I don't think you should say that about Jews."

"Oh," he said. "I didn't mean to offend you."

And I'm sure he didn't. So we left it. I was glad I let him know my response to his words, though still shaken by the way he had so easily let the slur slide out.

Being an ally takes many forms. Responding to slurs is one. Another is committing ourselves to working and living in non-segregated settings. People tend to hire people most like themselves. And live near people like themselves. And be friends with people like themselves. It seems natural and comfortable.

So it takes a bit of a push to extend ourselves, getting over some initial feelings of discomfort and confusion. What are the rules here? we wonder. And, Will I be accepted? Or liked? Is this unfamiliar way of doing things going to get the job done? It's a stretch.

In order to stretch this way and not pop, we need to be able to relax. If we make a mistake, well, so what? Most people will appreciate our intention. And if they don't, remember, the same thing has probably happened to them before and they lived through it. We will too. We will simply have learned something.

Being an Ally: To Ourselves

For those of us who have been long excluded, one of the people we need to be an ally to is ourselves. Even we who have been stereotyped begin to buy into the myths, believing we are not worthy. After all, there isn't a big shield around us, keeping us from hearing what we are "supposed" to be. And so we begin to act, or at least feel, as we are told we are.

One of our biggest tasks is to be able to see ourselves accurately, taking full credit for our accomplishments.

Even after all the years I have spent ridding myself of the limiting images of women, they still creep in. For instance, a few years ago when I was in Montana on my writing retreat, a young woman drove up to the ranch with my rental computer and printer.

Damn it, I thought. I wanted someone who could set this system up for me.

Only after she did a terrific job of getting everything hooked up did I realize how my age and gender stereotype had skewed my perception of her.

On another occasion recently, I walked into the office of the senior administrators of a hospital. I was there for a business meeting.

I arrived to find—two women! Neither one of them even had on a suit. Just skirts and blouses. It didn't seem quite real. How could they be in charge? They weren't very big, they weren't very old. They were a lot like me. How could they be running this hospital?

It's the old "I wouldn't want to be a member of any club that would have me as a member" syndrome. This manifests so frequently in organizations that provide advocacy for targeted people and are staffed by members of that group that it's become classic and predictable.

A large women's organization, doing ground-breaking work; organizational and personal trauma lasting for years. An African-American advocacy group, taking brilliant national leadership, self-de-structs. Why?

As the folk saying tells it, we have learned to pull down any other crab that tries to climb out of the barrel. "With friends like this, who needs enemies?"

The criticism we are so ready to give each other reflects the criticism we have received. How *can* we take ourselves seriously, when the world so rarely does?

Only recently, for example, have I taught myself to notice when I am viewing other female leaders through an unrealistic screen. That screen can take the form of an idealized image, leading to eventual disappoint-ment, or an overly critical one.

The messages about each excluded group's un-worthiness are so continual, and the variations on the theme so subtle, we really do drink them in with mother's milk.

The culture passes on these messages in lots of ways. Maybe our sister is favored because she has lighter skin and "better hair," or maybe it is the sons in our family who get help in going to college and the daughters don't get it, because they're "just going to get married anyway." Maybe it is learning that our Irish grandparents were despised as "uneducable." However it is delivered, we get the message: Our people, our gender, our class—we aren't worth much.

So we learn to doubt our capacity to excel. As women, for instance, even in that one arena that has been named ours—the reproduction of the species—who does it right?

Do we choose *not* to have children? We are selfish. If we do have children, and we are absorbed with their care, are we over-protective? Or, if we continue to live at the center of our own lives, are we neglectful? These doubts persist in the minds of most women, even in that one domain where we are supposed to shine.

When we do venture out, our abilities are constantly questioned by others, as well as ourselves. Our intelligence, our ability to command situations and people, our capacity to provide major national leadership, all these are still hotly debated. The common wisdom is that a woman—or a man of color—is still "unelectable," not only for the top job in the United States, but even for the second-in-command.

Those leaders from our group who do become visibly powerful suffer attacks and ridicule, which has the chilling effect of making many of us want to scurry for cover.

What can we do to more fully support our own and each others' leadership?

Notice the internalized message. When we feel the tug to distance ourselves from people in our group (because they're "too loud" or "too something") notice it, name it, and let it go.

Who cares if the stereotype is out there? In the words of my minister, the Reverend Eloise Oliver, "All the water in the ocean can't sink a ship, if the ship doesn't let it in."

We can take ourselves seriously and at the same time laugh at our mistakes. We get to make those too.

Appreciate each other. Point out skills, accomplishments, and effectiveness of actions. We need to hear specific appreciation from each other. We often don't know how much we have developed a strength until it is pointed out. Hearing the details assists our growth. We need these mirrors.

Notice our desires to trash our leaders, whether in our neighborhoods, workplaces, religious organizations, or our children's schools. Why do we feel so strongly that we must "correct" this situation by attacking? Are we feeling competitive, believing there is only room for one or two of "us"? Or are we so terrified about our urgent needs that we are unable to tolerate any mistakes by our leaders?

We *can* work our way out of the old images. Then

we will know that when we do stumble, friends will be there to pick us up, sending us on our way, stronger and wiser.

Checking Out
the Chairs at the Table

In addition to how we can support one another personally, we need to take a look at the larger social structures. As more people are coming to the table, we are finding we can't continue to serve the same old meal. We need to see what food, what kind of tables and which chairs fit for everyone and what needs to be changed, to allow for a diversity of styles and needs. Even the symbols that some of us took for granted—like the Confederate flag—aren't widely acceptable anymore.

A successful environment today needs to be an inclusive one. With different employees or students come different needs. As a nation we are undertaking a giant housecleaning in which everything is being reviewed. We are sorting out what is exclusionary and what we can keep, and figuring out how to put some of the new ways alongside the best of the old.

This is not an easy process. During this transition period, we need to be especially thoughtful all the way around.

It isn't always easy for "newcomers" to state their needs and perspectives on the dominant culture they are entering, so they should be asked. And it isn't always easy for those who have always run the club pretty much the same way, either. They are often afraid that things they care deeply about, like cherished holidays—or even their jobs—may be taken away from them.

The aspects of our lives which need to be examined are myriad.

Let's start with the simple chair.

They're usually too big, those conference room chairs at the meetings I go to. It's difficult to be the important person the others have come—perhaps driven hours or flown a day—to meet, and there I am. My feet barely touch the floor, my knees are unable to bend properly around the jutting front of the chair.

Or I sit boldly, confidently, feet planted firmly on the floor. And my bottom is six inches from the back of the chair, sliding perilously backward, if it's one of those slippery wooden chairs, rounded with arms. Unless I cramp my calves and grip the floor.

Who were these chairs built for anyway? Not executives like me, five-foot-four, 120 pounds fully dressed. A woman.

These chairs were built for men. Well, some men. Tall men. Large men, men who *should* be running companies and having high-level meetings in these impressive rooms. Talking of things that cost large amounts of money. Cutting million-dollar deals.

I've grown to enjoy these meetings, and have gotten good at making the deals. But almost always, the chairs don't fit. And so at these meetings I often comment on how the chairs are normed for men, and then I stand. Which does give me a certain commanding presence when I speak, standing, to a roomful of seated men.

I notice it is not only many women who don't fit these chairs. Anyone who is smaller than the average European-American man will be sliding and slipping. Anyone who is larger will be squeezed in between the arms.

If we are all to have seats at the table, they're going to have to come in a variety of sizes, including space for a wheelchair or two. How wonderful it will be for everyone to have a variety of chairs from which to choose. Certainly many European-American men also do not fit the current thrones.

Who Is a "Good Fit?"

Culture is composed of so many elements besides furniture and food: work and communication styles, music, clothing, pace, values, and more.

Employers and admissions committees recognize these as important when they speak of prospects as a "good fit." We all know something about it in our guts, when we enter a new place and look for the familiar cues that let us know we belong here. Part of becoming successfully diverse is naming these cues, these unwritten rules, and sorting through them. Whom do they make comfortable?

If some of the old ways are at cross-purposes with a new commitment to diversity, we are undercutting ourselves before we ever get going. If they support our newer missions, so much the better.

These questions are a beginning for self-examination. Reflecting on cultures we are part of gives us more insight into who might succeed in them—and why.

What is the language that is spoken? Literal and metaphoric? If people speak languages other than English, does that generate concern? What figures of speech are commonly used? To whom would they come easily? Whose class, gender, and ethnicity is represented in the images, the allusions, the references—to the books we are reading, our recreation and the vacations we take, the food we eat? These weren't questions when there was only one type of person in the workplace or school, and everyone spoke the same language—literally or figuratively.

What kinds of management/teaching styles are used? And which are recognized as best? A collaborative model, more associated, historically, with women and with some excluded ethnic groups? Or an individualistic model more associated with men?

What is the workplace norm for dress and grooming? What would or does happen if a woman of color shows up with her hair in braids? In dreadlocks? (Elaborate hair styles were common in many African cultures. Hair itself is a huge topic in African-American communities, since Black peoples' hair has long been a matter of great interest and concern to many European-Americans.) How are others supposed to wear their hair? What about beards? What are the norms on clothing—and for whom? For example, sometimes people of color feel they have to dress-up more, in order to get respect from white co-workers—or the local police.

What does one need to do to get ahead? Work fifty-hour weeks? Sixty? Are there the same expectations for mothers of young children? Fathers of young children? Is childcare provided? Flex time? In academia, are years to tenure flexible? And what research topics and styles are considered most valid?

Who has access to power? And how do they get access? On the golf course—at the country club that still doesn't admit people of color or single women? In the back office—where women are a rarity? At the business club luncheon? Among the guys going out for a beer after work? Jogging or tennis in the morning? Meetings?

How is networking done? Over backyard barbecues, lunch, professional meetings, clubs, religious organizations, bowling, schools once attended, neighborhoods? In other words, how did the people who wield power get there and stay there? Is there a process by which new people who didn't come through the old route are accepted into the "club"? Who is in the grapevine?

What jokes are acceptable? What is the norm for joking? If a person told an "Italian joke" what would be the likely response? Are there groups of people whom it is considered okay to jokingly demean? Women? Men? Large people? Short people? Gays?

What symbols are widely used, and how much diversity is tolerated? What posters, cartoons, or other art work? What would happen if someone put a poster of Malcolm X up in their office, dorm, or work space? Pink triangles? A swastika? How would any of these be greeted?

What is okay regarding sexual innuendo, "dirty" jokes, and sexual harassment? Can people put pin-ups on their locker doors? Office doors? Tell sexist jokes? Sexual jokes? What is the response if someone says he or she has been sexually harassed? Is there a clear grievance procedure?

How are same-gender relationships treated? Acknowl-edged? Is this different for men and women? Different for people at different levels or in different branches of the organization?

Whose contributions are valued, and how does that manifest? What is the forum in which this occurs? Is there some mechanism (for example, a staff meeting, a suggestion box, individual conferences) through which contributions can be made? And once made, whose voices are valued?

These questions are limited only by your endurance and imagination.

Every aspect of daily life is part of your organizational culture: the books, newspapers, or magazines which are there, the way people are addressed, the reward and punishment systems, the lunches that are eaten, the pace of work, and on and on. Every one of these areas matters to everyone in the organization, even if they are not consciously aware of each one.

As workplaces and schools include more people who formerly were not there, clashes begin to occur. And confusion.

What is sexual or racial harassment? These weren't big issues a generation ago, although both occurred. In 1961, for example, when one of my favorite English-literature professors asked me to sleep with him, I had no concept of sexual harassment. I was simply stunned, couldn't quite believe I had heard correctly, and fled.

We didn't have names for harassment then and laws prohibiting it. Those behaviors were just "life." Now that the rules are changing, the definitions of appropriate behavior are still being worked out.

Even decision-making processes are being newly examined. How can people making decisions solicit many points of view and still not have a cumbersome process? This is not a new question, but it takes on another meaning as more diverse perspectives are included.

It has been demonstrated repeatedly that the more people in a workplace or team experience respect, the more creative, fully engaged and productive they are. It pays to examine the unwritten rules—all those invisible components of climate and culture.

The Menu

Every organization has written policies and procedures—the advertised menu of the meal. These need to be examined in the same way as the unwritten rules are, for they also define who is in and who is out.

Some examples:

Holiday time-off policy. Many people are excluded from current policies, because major Christian religious holidays are typically scheduled as time off, whereas Jewish, Buddhist, Muslim, and other religious and cultural holidays rarely are. Usually people from those groups need to use personal or vacation days to observe their cultural or religious holidays, if that option is available.

This is an example of a uniform policy with a differential impact. It depends who you are whether your holiday is included in the "official list," which in turn determines how much discretionary vacation time you have at your disposal. It may be difficult to ask to use even vacation or personal time for this purpose. Employers have various responses. I have heard reports of, "If you're not here Monday, don't come Tuesday," and more subtle but still disapproving responses—as well as employers who make every effort to accommodate a range of cultural and religious observances.

Some organizations have resolved this dilemma by having several days designated as "floating holidays," to be used as desired for observance of holidays such as Three Kings Day, Boxing Day, Kwanzaa, Rosh Hoshana, Yom Kippur, Chinese New Year, or Divali.

Family benefits. When "family" includes only people legally affiliated, this, like the holiday policy, has differential impact. People excluded are those who still cannot legally marry their same-sex partners— just as biracial couples could not until 1967 in many states. Family benefits can be substantial: discounted air fares, medical benefits, use of health club facilities, and a wide array of other delectable perks.

Some corporations and universities—such as Lotus Development Corporation, Silicon Graphics, Levi Strauss & Co., Stanford and Columbia universities, and Georgia State—have broadened their benefits packages to include same-gender partners. This is a trend that undoubtedly will continue.

Sexual harassment policies. Do you know if your workplace or school has one? If so, do you know what it is, how to use it, and who to talk to if you need it? One of the major problems with these policies is that few people have any idea what they are. They may or may not have been handed the policy with their new student or new employee orientation packet, but two years later who knows where it is? Or what it is?

Wheelchair accessibility of offices or meeting sites is sometimes a stated requirement. Who has access to a shop floor, an office, a classroom, or a meeting place? This is the most literal of inclusions/exclusions.

Reward systems. Are efforts to successfully diversify considered important enough to gain (or lose) points when it counts—at promotion time? Unless they are, rhetoric about change will be greeted politely, at best.

Examining the current policies and procedures is a process and takes time. Yet even the change process itself is an opportunity to be inclusive and to engage people in the creation of their environments. This is the work in which our culture is now engaged. We are engaged at it on many levels and in many forms. Of course culture is always evolving, so this is not totally new. But the breadth of the change we are undergoing right now is unusual. Thus the depth of the conflict.

5

Top Ten Plus Two:
Questions About Diversity

What about telling jokes? Isn't humor healthy? I learned my best "Polish jokes" from a Pole and my best "Mexican jokes" from a Chicano.

Humor is one of life's greatest gifts, bringing laughter and joy. It is also sometimes used to justify and reinforce differences in power. It can serve to "put people in their place"—at the foot of the table—because of a supposed group characteristic.

It seems that once the label "joke" is put on a statement, anything goes. When we are uncomfortable and protest, we are often met with, "What's the matter, can't you take a joke? Where's your sense of humor? Lighten up."

To which we may respond: "My sense of humor is still waiting for something funny to be said."

Sometimes oppressive humor is justified by the

logic that members of the target group use the same joke—or the same stereotype—themselves. This in-group humor, in which we name our own exaggerated characteristics (sometimes our survival mechanisms) and laugh at them, is a different kettle of fish. It's similar to talking badly about our family—and having someone else do it. The same remark takes on a completely different meaning.

An example of in-group humor which relies on a stereotype:

"How many lesbians does it take to replace a light bulb?"

"Six. One to put in the bulb, five to process it."

In this case, the stereotype is that lesbians, in our zeal for egalitarian groups, process every action forever. As a lesbian, I find it funny, but wouldn't appreciate heterosexuals telling it. Then I'm the butt of the humor. If I tell it, I'm laughing affectionately at my group's (and my own) foible. The wit, for me, provides some perspective.

Assessing the helpfulness of such humor is a matter of context and judgment. Not everyone within a culture agrees that self-deprecating humor is ever healing. Some believe that this serves to reinforce a group's own negative self-image. There is wide debate on this within cultures.

So, best not to mess with it if you are outside the group.

If someone else outside a group does get into it and

you are uncomfortable, you can always say you don't like it—and why, if that's appropriate. The nature of your response will vary according to your relationship to the speaker, the setting, how strongly you feel, who else is around, and your own style. I've seen effective responses range from a short, light-hearted "Yuck," accompanied by mimed gagging, to carefully thought-out written statements about where we are as a society on these issues, and everything in between: Questioning the speaker about motivation ("Why are you saying this?"); leaving the situation, with or without comment; taking someone aside later to express misgivings about the "joke"—and at the same time expressing personal support. Each of these very different techniques can be effective in registering discomfort and opening a dialogue about the implications of humor that relies for its "bite" on the degradation of somebody. Usually somebody else.

When should I mention the race of a person? Always... never?

It depends on several things. Such as whether you are a member of the group in question and who your audience is. It also depends, like most things in life, on context.

For example, if you say, "There was a Chinese guy standing on the corner waiting for a taxi when . . .," are you including his ethnicity because it is relevant to what happened next? Was someone reacting to him because of his ethnicity? Are you a member of the group, speaking about a brother? If so, that carries a completely different meaning than someone who is outside the group describing him that way.

For the rest of us, mentioning ethnicity unless it is relevant is usually not helpful, because ethnicity is such a charged topic in the United States, and because there are so many unflattering stereotypes floating around.

On the other hand, never mentioning an ethnic designator, and stubbornly refusing to acknowledge group membership (usually out of an attempt to be non-prejudicial) can also be offensive and seen as willfully ignoring an individual's culture.

Sometimes educators in seminars tell me, "I don't know how many of my students are Black or white. I don't notice race." This is simply ignoring one key— not the only one—to the students they interact with. It also seems patently untrue, in this culture, to not "notice" race.

So, think about when ethnicity is relevant. Don't shy away from it when it is; don't introduce it when it isn't. It's one of those situations in which we need to keep opposite ideas in mind simultaneously, something most of us Westerners aren't too good at yet.

As Pat Parker, the late African-American lesbian poet, wrote:

FOR THE WHITE PERSON WHO WANTS TO KNOW HOW TO BE MY FRIEND

The first thing you do is to forget that I'm Black. Second, you must never forget that I'm Black. You should be able to dig Aretha, but don't play her every time I come over. And if you decide to play Beethoven—don't tell me his life story. They made us take music appreciation too.

Eat soul food if you like it, but don't expect me to locate your restaurants or cook it for you.

And if some Black person insults you, mugs you, rapes your sister, rapes you, rips off your house or is just being an ass--please, do not apologize to me for wanting to do them bodily harm. It makes me wonder if you're foolish.

And even if you really believe Blacks are better lovers than whites—don't tell me. I start thinking of charging stud fees.

In other words—if you really want to be my friend— don't make a labor of it. I'm lazy. Remember.

Why do groups keep changing their names? I never know what to say. So, for fear of offending, I don't say much.

Groups change their names because history changes. *African-American*, for instance, became a desirable term in the U.S. following the independence of many African nations from colonial relationships.

And consciousness changes. *Asian-American* and *Pacific Islander* came into popular use a few years ago in reaction to *Oriental*, a word coined by Europeans. Yet, as with other terms which designate entire regions or continents (like *European-American*), many peoples' first identity is a national one. For example, Filipino, Vietnamese, or Japanese-American.

Sixty percent of the world's population is Asian, comprising vastly different nationalities, so lumping them all together into one category is a stretch. Most first- and second-generation Asian-Americans refer to themselves by country of origin, unless they are making general statements about all Asian-Americans. The same is true with Native Americans: Individuals often refer to themselves or each other by one of the more than five hundred tribal designations, unless discussing general situations of all Native Americans.

Women became the term most adult females came to prefer as we raised our own awareness about the less-than-adult legal and cultural status women had, all reflected in the word *girl*. The word had a special history too, from its particular use to describe women of color, similar to *boy* for men of color. As we seek to put that history behind us, we understandably look for new designations.

How can we recruit a diverse team when we can't find any qualified "minorities" or women out there? Everybody wants them.

When the search committee comes back and says the only qualified candidates they could turn up were white males, they simply haven't known where to look. Or how to see past their own screen of old images.

For example, the president of a major university recently told me of such a result in a vice presidential search, although he had instructed both the search committee and a consulting firm that he wanted a diverse candidate pool. When he got on the phone with the consulting firm and told them they wouldn't be paid unless they complied with his instructions, they did. The next morning he had on his desk the resumes of two outstanding "unconventional" candidates—as he called them—to add to the pool. One of them ended up getting the job.

There are lots of ways to recruit under represented people. It means developing new networks—which takes lots of time and some money—and planning ahead by, for instance, inviting promising people in for visits well before graduation, providing loan reductions, or various in-house development efforts. And creating an inviting atmosphere, both for recruitment, and its twin, retention.

It also means examining the screens we may unconsciously be using, which tend to filter out folks much different than ourselves. It is easy to forget that people express brilliance in a variety of ways, as well as the chilling effect the environment may be having, even during the interview process.

What about "reverse discrimination?" And affirmative action?

Timing is everything in life, some people say. To which I would add, context.

Everybody, unfortunately, seems to be capable of prejudice: stereotyping members of our own and other groups, and acting on it.

Some people have the clout to enforce those prejudices widely, creating whole systems based on them. For example: slavery, legal prohibitions against women entering into contracts, keeping lesbians and gay men out of some occupations, steering prospective home buyers of color to certain neighborhoods. That's discrimination.

Sometimes these systems are invisible, based on unwritten rules. Other times they are implemented through codes, such as the one discovered recently at a major retail chain, which coded the apparent race of shoppers in order to determine whose checks would be cashed. Or point systems such as the one described to me at a business leaders' seminar in Detroit: Prospective buyers in a fashionable suburb were, this resident told me, until very recently ascribed points based on race, religion, occupation, and class. (Most people didn't make it.)

Because these systems and more have existed for so long, we have all gotten used to a kind of invisible "tracking," even when the formal codes are dismantled. We've had to create procedures to try to compensate for our unconscious perpetuation of the old practices. Hopefully these are temporary ones that will help us normalize relationships.

Why is there no white student union or special program at my job for whites? So many resources go to special-interest groups.

Most corporations, government agencies, and educational institutions are directed by whites, who typically re-create their own culture and fill the institutions, especially at senior levels, with other people much like themselves. The overall environment is itself a "special (white) program," merely invisible because it is so prevalent.

In an attempt to create climates, cultures, and curricula that include others, programs are created to support the change. We've found over the past generation that just opening the doors and saying, "Okay, now you can come in," doesn't work very well. The climate and structures usually don't accommodate diverse viewpoints, interests, and needs; the newcomers tend to feel isolated and leave. Thus, "special programs" for "special-interest groups": 75 percent of the population (overlapping groups of women, people of color, and lesbians and gay men). Hopefully such programs are transitional, leading to the time when inclusive environments are business as usual and become self-sustaining.

Meanwhile, lots of people in the more advantaged group (whites or males) aren't having such an easy time of it, either. So the larger task is creating environments that will support everyone. In fact, sometimes programs initiated for "minorities" are, when proven successful, taken campus-wide or company-wide. This is a useful model in that the groups experiencing the greatest need are getting the pilot programs. Everyone indirectly benefits right from the beginning when the "special programs" contribute to more harmonious and productive environments. And everyone directly benefits in the end, by having access to the programs.

Aren't stereotypes pretty much based on truth?

Some stereotypes, like the alleged mental inferiority of one gender or racial group, or the belief that another group has horns—yes, this has been believed—are made of whole cloth. Other stereotypes are based on an observable characteristic of some people in a group—often a condition they have been forced or tracked into—and as such, may have bits of truth. The problem is that when we try to apply that bit of truth to random people we meet, chances are, it won't fit.

It is fascinating to study the origin of stereotypes. They provide insight into a group's history and its intersection with the dominant culture. But using the stereotype to try to understand someone's behavior, or predict it, usually won't work.

There is a subtle difference here between a stereotype and history. Learning about the history of, say, Cambodians, may provide me with a helpful backdrop into which I can place a Cambodian person I meet. It may enrich my understanding of her. But it will rarely predict her behavior accurately. As baseball great Casey Stengal is reputed to have said, "Prediction isn't difficult. It's only when it's about the future that it doesn't work."

Why do all the Blacks (or Chicanos, or other people of color) sit together in the cafeteria?

This is a question of both perception and safety. It's amazing how selectively we perceive situations. For instance, a friend told me the following story. She, an African-American woman, was teaching a college class on racism. The course had fourteen students: six were people of color. One of the requirements of the course was to keep a journal, to be turned in periodically. Mid-semester, one of the white students wrote, "This is the first time I've ever been in a class where the *majority* of students are people of color."

I've noticed making similar mental slips myself, and have come to realize this is a common response to a group of "others." They often seem more numerous and more monolithic than they are. They are also especially visible in a sea of "us." So, we notice the few people of color, or the two women in senior ranks, but not the more numerous whites in the cafeteria, or white males at the top. People rarely ask, "Why are all the whites eating together?"

It may be, in fact, that *all* of the Chicanos or Haitians aren't sitting over there. Maybe four friends are eating together.

And then there is safety. Often members of a group who are commonly stereotyped, or excluded from the majority group's social networks, enjoy an opportunity to be with other group members. The easy familiarity—not having to be on guard for hostility, not having to educate, the shared culture, the fun—there are lots of reasons it may seem easier to stick close to home. If this is frequently the case, it's one indicator about the overall climate. Some people may be finding it a bit chilly. That's the thing to focus on: What can you do to warm up the climate?

When I see a blind person about to cross a street, or a person in a wheelchair struggling up a hill, should I help them?

Rule Number one: Observe for a moment. Rule number two: Ask. Rule number three: Be sure to ask.

If you do determine help might be useful and you ask, "Would you like a hand?" responses will vary. Many people, I've found, respond with an appreciative, "Yes, thank you." Then after I've gotten instruction about what to do, I can let someone take my arm, if that's what is wanted, or give the wheelchair a gentle push, with as little intrusion into their physical space as I would to a sighted or standing person.

The reason for two of the three rules being "Ask" is that people with disabilities, like children and women, often find their personal space violated with no warning. As adults are quick to pick up children, pinch them, squeeze them, and kiss them—even when they are total strangers—with no permission asked or given, so are able-bodied people quick to zoom into the space of a person with a disability. (As a woman, I have experienced a similarly casual male entry into my space, groped on the subway or street, even kissed on the lips suddenly by men with whom I have been friends.)

When you ask people with a disability whether they would like assistance, sometimes you may get a no, either because they are quite capable of getting across the street or up the hill without assistance, or because they're just furious at the world (and you as its representative) that day, which may or may not have anything to do with their disability.

You never know what kind of answer you'll get when you ask, but there is usually appreciation for your having had the courtesy to ask. You recognized the person underneath the disability, a person who doesn't want his or her space invaded any more than you would if, as a sighted person, a stranger suddenly took your arm as you were about to cross a busy street and started to pull you across.

What about the Christmas party? I've always had a small Christmas tree on my desk, and now I'm told it offends a few people. That's my favorite time of year. What shall I do? Can't we have any fun anymore?

Yes, you can have fun. In fact, it might be fine to have your desk Christmas tree, so long as other types of holiday symbols are simultaneously welcome and visible.

The former office "Christmas party" has been replaced by the "holiday party" at many locations. The problem with this, if that's all that's done, is that Christmas, a Christian holiday, is such a major focus of our entire culture for the month of December. It's

hard to keep its symbolism from dominating everything, precipitating a December dilemma for many
people. If you want to publicly celebrate Christmas, it
is important to think carefully about how to include
other cultural/religious symbols at the same time.

One organization I consulted with decided that the
company would provide a range of holiday symbols
for employee use. They had small Christmas trees,
Kwanzaa murals and corn, menorahs (although Ha-
nukkah is not a major Jewish holiday), and symbols of
the winter solstice—all holidays falling within a week
or two of each other in December. These were all
displayed in a low-key manner, there was a small
holiday party in the third week of December, and most
employees were satisfied.

Another organization, which had a food drive for
shelters every Christmas, changed its policy to rotate
the drive every third year among three major holidays
observed by its staff: Christmas, Pesach (Passover),
and Chinese New Year—giving visibility to the last
two major holidays.

*Why is it such a big deal if historical symbols are
used which some people now object to, like the
Confederate flag or the Canadian national an-
them? We can't go around and change all of our
cherished symbols from the past.*

If these cherished symbols are still in use then they're having an impact today.

The Confederate flag was a symbol of slavery. As such, it is a painful remnant of a terrible time, and is interpreted by many today as a symbol of wishing to recall segregation. Some people who use the flag aren't conscious of that interpretation. It's just part of their familiar, and valued, landscape. Yet because of its history, the flag has a huge impact on many viewers, who are all too conscious of the association.

In the Canadian example, half of the population is effectively excluded when "O Canada" is sung every morning in public schools, with its reference to "true patriot love in all thy sons command"—and no mention of daughters. Thus the change proposed in a House of Commons bill to "in all our hearts command."

Negotiating the new menu that will include everyone is a delicate matter. Most of us resist change in some ways, while others, conscious of exclusion, are pushing it. Fortunately, many of the changes we think will be so devastating turn out to feel like normal life well before we could have imagined.

I remember so many white people in the 1960s who really thought they might die if they had to eat with, work with, or share a bathroom with a person of color. Yet I didn't notice the death rate of whites rising after integration.

We humans are surprisingly flexible creatures.

Where does "diversity" stop? Are we going to have to protect and "value" child molesters or Nazis? Where do we draw the line?

Our culture has drawn the line differently at different times. For instance, in the 1950s and early 1960s, "civil rights" meant rights for African-Americans. Period. "Sex" was added as a joke, in a rider to the Civil Rights Act of 1964, by conservative senators who hoped to defeat the bill with this outlandish addition. But it passed. And gave a legal leg-up to this wave of the women's equity movement that arrived a few years later.

Including gender in "diversity" seemed like a huge stretch then. As did including the concerns of other people of color. Now, many institutions routinely include a variety of groups in their definition of the diversity they wish to affirm: women and several groups (at least) of people of color, gay men, lesbians, people with disabilities, and religious minorities.

What about the practical impact of including "everyone"? How much will it cost, for instance, to have health benefits for all partners who wish them, or "reasonable accommodations" for people with differing physical or mental abilities? Actual costs have typically turned out to be significantly less than the range that has been feared. The "What About Me?" syndrome has been avoided, and the talent pool has been enlarged.

Who gets a seat at the table is differently determined each generation. Child molesters? Nazis? We can affirm the rights of people to treatment or free speech without suggesting that they are members of targeted populations that deserve the status of "protected minorities."

Who has "protected" legal status is a shifting issue. At one time or another, most everybody in our history didn't have much standing in the eyes of the law. White men without property, for instance, being unable to vote, had few legal rights when the United States was formed. Women, Asian-Americans, Latinos/Latinas, African-Americans, Native Americans—each group has battled to get a seat. People with disabilities were laughed at when they and their allies raised issues of accessibility and discrimination only fifteen years ago. And now we have the 1992 Americans with Disabilities Act, assuring a variety of civil rights. Gay men and lesbians are today in the position that many other groups have been in before, with our "rights" being contested state by state, as well as in national arenas such as the military.

Where we "draw the line," whether we have to, and how we do it, is indeed one of the great questions of our day—as slavery and women's rights were in the mid-nineteenth century.

6

Diversity, Why Bother?

There is so much to worry about these days with the economy, how can we think about diversity, too? Isn't our plate—and the table—full enough?

Of course, this is the time when we need to think about it the most. Because the human mind just seems to slip into scapegoating mode whenever the economy gives enough people a hard ride. Problems? It must be the fault of the . . . (different names in different eras; today it's "immigrants.")

And during rough times, "last hired, first fired" means that diversity is on a collision course with another hard-won principle: seniority. So if we don't take on the whole topic, we really are going to splinter. There's no choice anymore.

As a nation, we have a good shot at taking global leadership on this one. We've got the mix, we've got the experience, and we have an increasing commitment from every sector of society.

Yet one of the barriers to success is that diversity, when not seen as altogether irrelevant, is often viewed as something legally or politically necessary—and possibly morally good—but which will lower standards and quality. This notion is not surprising, because it expresses the very belief that kept people out of organizations in the first place: Difference equals weakness or inferiority. Rather than: Difference equals added value.

Standards: Aren't They Rising?

Bringing more people to the welcome table has stimulated much discussion of "standards" and fears about whether quality will be sacrificed. This question has a certain irony in that there is simultaneous wide recognition of the superior capabilities often required for a man of color or a woman—who has to be "twice as good"—to rise anywhere near the top of most corporations or academic institutions.

But whoever said logic had anything to do with all of this?

"Standards" are often flung about as if they are immutable, with no questions asked. Yet, I often wonder, whose standards is it we are upholding? How did they come to be? And what constitutes the excellence we are so insistent on keeping?

In academia, for example, the written word rules.

The more abstract the concept, the greater the prestige. Quantitative analysis—using numbers—is considered more rigorous and more valid than qualitative analysis, with its case studies, field work, and anecdotal evidence. This standard describes one way of representing knowledge, which its proponents have had enough clout to call "truth."

Less value is given to strengths particularly developed in the rest of us. For example, communication skills, problem-solving styles that use multifaceted approaches, and an ethic that features a strong sense of responsibility to community and "giving back."

People in excluded groups have, of course, developed skills in other areas as well, as have some white men become proficient in, say, inter-disciplinary approaches. One of the joys of knowledge is that it is not culture-bound. It is simply often generated in a culturally specific manner, since people develop ways of thinking to accommodate particular environments.

Many women, for instance, have been socialized to work interactively, to share power and information, and to promote empowerment of others—students, subordinates, and colleagues. Men, on the other hand, often use a military organizational model, with its hierarchy of command, and a different form of bonding. Women are typically more process oriented and more tolerant of ambiguity than men, perhaps because the daily life in which we are often mired is itself ambiguous, without neat beginnings or endings. We sometimes are spoken of as thinking in webs, intricately, rather than in straight lines. To men conditioned to linear thinking, this can look like chaos. To those of us conditioned, in household labor, to think of six things at once—from multiple viewpoints—their thinking can appear simplistic.

An example of differential perceptions and how they affect research was described by Dr. Meredith Burke to the Institute for Women's Policy Research Conference in 1990. Two groups of U.S. economists conducted research in Jamaica during 1978 for the Interamerican Development Bank. In order to make recommendations, the economists needed to estimate the unemployment rate. The male-only team estimated it at 11 to 12 percent. The mixed-gender group of economists had a startlingly different finding, later determined to be accurate: 35 percent unemployment. The reason for the discrepancy? The male team subtracted from the numbers of unemployed all mothers of young children, assuming they were unavailable. The male economists failed to discover a piece of data a female economist on the second team found: a widespread network of informal child-care arrangements.

The men's experiences had not prepared them to read all of the variables in the situation accurately, leading them to an incorrect assessment of a vital statistic upon which critical economic policy recommendations depended. Someday the female economist's method of gathering data may be analyzed so it can become part of the education—and the evaluation—of all future economists.

Another example of the wisdom different groups bring arose in July 1993. Major news media reported on a new piece of surprising data: Never-married women were found to be having babies at twice the rate of a decade before, rising to 24 percent of all never-married women. The analysts of this census data were reported to be somewhat puzzled, speculating only that the "breakdown of the family" contributed. Any lesbian could have told them—had she been on the team—that the lesbian baby boom of the 1980s and 1990s, a topic of much discussion in the lesbian community, was probably responsible for much of it. It is the first explanation that would have occurred to most lesbians: Lesbians are a large part of "never-married women," lesbians until the 1980s rarely had children outside of heterosexual marriages, there has been enormous pent-up demand, and now the mores have changed. Hence, a lesbian baby boom.

The potential contribution of formerly excluded groups was brought home to me personally one evening.

I went to my local Emergency Room suffering from acute chest pain. I knew that it was bronchial because I'd been having a tickling in my throat for a few days. The pain was rapidly moving down my chest, and was so alarming that I needed to rule out pneumonia. My own doctor suggested on the telephone that I not wait until morning.

When I first saw a medical person and began to describe my symptoms, he immediately suspected heart attack. I knew it wasn't that because of the way this had developed over the last few days from a sore throat, but I accepted their need to cover all bases.

So I had my EKG. Normal.

Next the physician checked my lungs. He didn't hear anything and therefore ruled out any problem having to do with lungs.

His conclusion: I had strained my chest muscle "doing something" and I shouldn't exert for a few days. I demurred, telling him, again, the brief history of the pain. He allowed as how it couldn't be lungs because the "lungs were clear" (to his inspection) and patiently reiterated why, since he had ruled out heart and lungs, it *had* to be chest muscle.

This diagnosis was demonstrated to be incorrect when I developed full-blown bronchitis a few days later.

Given the battery of tests I went through, this erroneous conclusion by a "good" clinician at a highly regarded facility cost several thousand dollars and many hours of wasted time. And why did he make that incorrect diagnosis? Because he wasn't *listening* to me. Although he treated me with personal respect, he did not respect my knowledge of and accuracy about reporting my own body's condition. That factor was not valued highly in his system of observation.

I pondered this on my trip home. If standards were expanded in medicine to include the ability to listen carefully, I thought, better treatment would result from more accurate diagnoses. Thus the quality of medical care would improve and the overall standards rise. There simply needs to be a way to teach and assess excellence in listening.

It happens that listening is a skill at which those of us who have been subordinated are often adept. We've had to listen well in order to attend properly to those upon whom our fate depends. Additionally, for women of all ethnic groups, training in listening is part of the conditioning to be nurturers.

In the last twenty years, enough of us who had been excluded from academia have been let in that we have been expanding the boundaries of research— even the concept of what constitutes evidence. There is a new wave of scholarship that integrates many layers of experience, including personal ones, in investigating a topic.

In the field of history, for instance, until recently only written or material evidence was considered valid. Yet those of us who did not create the current "standards" often have a vast heritage of oral history. African-Americans, for example, were cut off from the traditional recording systems of their ancestors by being forcibly separated from people who spoke their language, and then were legally prohibited from literacy for several hundred years. Women of all ethnicities have been denied access to "formal" scholarship for much of history.

Many cultures have developed strong oral traditions, using song, dance and poetry as well as narrative to record their stories. In the last generation it has primarily been descendants of these people who have resurrected these traditions. By doing so they are providing a fuller picture of all U.S. history. They are also enriching written tradition by adding other communication styles that incorporate subtleties beyond the capabilities of the written word. When only written documents were perceived as evidence, a great deal was lost.

Also, in higher education, faculty isolation has recently been identified as a major problem. The individual research model doesn't foster cooperation, but rather encourages competition. This creates low morale, decreased productivity and eventually exhaustion for many scholars. To combat this some institutions are putting considerable effort into promoting a greater sense of community. There are discussions of strengthening "teams" as a way of strengthening scholarship, as well as an effort by educators nationwide to promote a more collegial approach to learning.

An interesting source for a counterpoint to the ethic of individualism might be the community values of many Latinos/Latinas, African-Americans, Native

Americans, and Asian-Americans. There is a strong historic ethic in each of these communities which puts community before the individual. This ethic has not been highly valued by the dominant Anglo-European-American culture thus far, nor has it been perceived as an ethic contributing to scholarship.

The idea that standards could be expanded to include more of the strengths developed by more groups of people and thus create stronger institutions, with higher quality, seems obvious. Yet it has not been greeted warmly by some. This resistance was expressed a few years ago at Yale University via a flyer plastering the campus.

It said only:

WAR IS PEACE

LIES ARE TRUTH

DIVERSITY IS EXCELLENCE

Yet our different positions in society have provided us with different viewpoints and skills. Fortunately for the expansion of our knowledge base, we all have the capacity to learn a wide range of skills and methods, once they are recognized as valuable.

As we enter the era now two generations removed from legal discrimination by race and gender, it is time to give honored places at the table to people who utilize various methods of scholarship. Doing so will encourage more creative thinking and greater possibilities for the generation of new knowledge and new methods of problem solving, gifts not to be tossed off lightly.

Variety is the Spice of Life

In our newsrooms, as well as at universities, an exclusion of diverse viewpoints has lowered quality. For example, Asian-Americans and Latinos/Latinas are often not assigned to bilingual-education stories—because of possible "bias." Journalists who are openly lesbian or gay are frequently asked these days not to report on stories that involve lesbians or gays—bias again. Other ethnic minority groups are discovering the same closed doors.

Yet heterosexual white men have never been asked not to cover Congress, which contains so many of "their" group. They were never kept off stories involving other white male clubs—the Pentagon or Wall Street—because of possible bias. There have been so many of them on both sides of the media camera that their presence simply looks normal and therefore, "objective."

Now that the rest of us have gotten a foot (and sometimes a whole body) in the media door, questions are raised about our professional abilities.

Treating "special interests" differently in journalism is nothing new. At one point all that women could write was the "women's page." Every African-American was an expert on Martin Luther King, Jr., presumed to know about nothing but race.

Now the pendulum is swinging to the other extreme: exclusion from "our" topics.

Those who have been overrepresented in media, with more than 90 percent of the decision-making seats, have never been more "objective" than anyone else. They have simply been so numerous that they've had the power to call their biases reality.

Well, it isn't so. Every human—including that "universal (white) man"—has a point of view. Hopefully, as we grow, we each stretch our vision so that we can see ever more of the picture. But it's always one set of eyes, one brain, one life carrying the message about what we see. Each of our messages are therefore different.

And we need all of them to form a complete text.

In the political arena as well, diversity encourages excellence. During the last few presidential campaigns, none-of-the-above has been the voters' candidate of choice.

Among other aspects, all of the nationally recognized candidates seemed to share several startling similarities: their race, their gender, and their apparent sexual orientation.

The heterosexual-white-male model may have been a good idea at one time, but it's gone stale as the *only* game in town. When a sports team uses the same play repeatedly during the game, its effectiveness declines. Likewise with this rerun.

The candidates each season have been limited as a group, in that they represent such a narrow range of possible life experiences and perspectives. It's as if only one food choice were available to us, as consumers. Our bodies could not sustain themselves on this homogeneous diet, no matter how excellent the one item was. Likewise with the body politic. We need variety to thrive.

Their striking similarities prevent the candidates from sharpening and developing their own thinking as they would need to were they pressured by significant differences among the candidate pool.

Common sense indicates that the larger and more diverse the pool, the larger the chance of finding great talent, fresh perspectives and creative solutions. Nature flourishes on diversity. In genetics, without a diverse pool the species degenerates. In a presidential race, without a diverse pool of candidates, the level of discourse degenerates.

In business as in politics, the greater the diversity, the greater the possibility of finding an array of skills. By the year 2000, 85 percent of the net new work force will be those so long considered "others." A business that is not set up to provide a hospitable environment will be unable to retain people very long. And the costs of the revolving door are high: hiring and training a new worker has been estimated at costing half to the full amount of their annual salary.

One management executive told me that he thought women often brought skills to project management which he saw less frequently in men. My client thought it was because women had been socialized to value skills in human relations, as they have taken leadership in family and community life. Many women, he said, use each other as resources more easily than men—and have something to teach at a time when businesses are grappling with working in networks. On the other hand, he observed, many men have been more conditioned to be aggressive, to not settle for less than the full price asked, and to be tough in a variety of ways, different than women's toughness.

Bringing these two sets of conditioning together can cause conflict. But, if well understood and managed, the team can provide a terrifically well-rounded array of talent. And each group can learn skills from the other.

Corporations selling everything from automobiles to cosmetics, sneakers to real estate, are discovering that ads and sales forces tuned in to previously ignored cultures are increasing market share. Chevrolet, Avon, and Nike have each improved sales based on specific campaigns pitched to targeted population segments—whom they need to understand in order to reach. Real estate firms in California are hiring agents who speak Cantonese, Mandarin, Japanese, Tagalog, or other languages, and who understand the nuances of several cultures. And it is paying off.

A few years ago when my partner and I were home-shopping, I asked a real estate broker on the telephone if the firm had any openly lesbian agents. I thought it would be more comfortable for us. I had been on the road, was exhausted, and simply didn't want any hassle that day, nor did I feel like doing education on my time off. (Sometimes well-meaning but uncomfortable allies can be tediously curious, as in, "How do your children feel about your relationship?" and on to other personal questions.)

The broker I spoke with was sent into a complete panic by my question. The next day she insisted on visiting my office with the firm's owners, whereupon I gradually understood that they were afraid I was a government screener, sent to ask them this "trick question," which they didn't know how to answer correctly. (So much for no hassle.)

Perhaps today the intent of the question—and my own obvious misadventures with previous agents—might be better understood.

Because the benefits of diversity have not long been obvious, many of the formerly excluded have long tried to assimilate to the dominant norms. We ourselves are only now beginning to understand how fully we provide "value added."

Variety may be not only the spice of life, but the meat as well. Or the tofu, depending on your preference.

Viva la Diferencia!

Every targeted U.S. minority group has attempted, as part of its civil rights struggle, to demonstrate to the majority population that its members are similar in their humanity to others. There is the understandable desire to show that we are much like you, you who have power. Power to set the norms of culture, language, and standards. Power to let us in or keep us out.

Thus, in the early years of the Black civil rights movement, we always dressed in suits and dresses when on picket lines. We wanted to show America how normal, how respectable, and how worthy of a seat at the table everyone was. I remember in 1961 how dressed-up we all were when we picketed Woolworth's in New Haven with the NAACP. (This didn't make any difference when I invited the whole crowd, about twenty-five people, back to my apartment for a party after the picketing was over. The police arrived within fifteen minutes to eject the party-goers from my all-white building, and I was evicted the next day.)

The refrain throughout the history of the African-American struggle for justice on these shores has been: "Ain't I a woman?" (Sojourner Truth) and "I am a man," "I bleed too, just like you."

Likewise the women's movement has insisted that we too have the capacity to perform physical and mental labor *equal to men.*

And now the gay rights movement has made a serious effort to mainstream our message, to present ourselves as "the girl (or boy) next door."

It all makes sense politically, given the stereotypes that targeted groups have had to live down and live around. And, it's even true. In fact, it's why gays and lesbians are often invisible. In so many ways we are all strikingly similar, we are all "normal"; and it will be helpful to the attainment of our political and civil rights to be acknowledged as such.

Yet, this assimilationist/girl-next-door message misses something. For part of the wonder of this universe we inhabit is the special spirit and unique culture that each group brings to the table. That special quality goes by a variety of names—soul, *chutzpah*, feminine intuition, *alma*, gay spirit. Whatever you call it, it needs to be noted and cherished.

Every group ought to be recognized for its unique contribution, rather than being perceived as "sad copies of the original," as an editorial writer recently characterized gay couples. In fact, we "copies," while often presenting ourselves publicly—and truthfully— as victimized by restrictive social policy, often express our relief privately at having escaped the confines of dominant-group convention.

As any group moves toward greater inclusion, it faces a persistent tension between the desire to assert commonality and the desire to maintain, indeed to celebrate, that which makes us different. As a saying about immigrants has it: The first generation retains the ways of the old country. The second generation wants desperately to assimilate, forget the old ways and be completely "American." The third generation asks, "Where are my roots? Who am I, and what makes me special?"

The public existence of gays and lesbians today is between the second and third generations, with the resultant tension between the two perspectives.

The 1993 March on Washington was a delightful reminder to cherish gay humor, our campy ways, our fun, our flaunting of rigid gender roles.

To wit:

In the contingent of religious groups, marching behind Mormon Brethren, Catholics, Baptists and Unitarians, was a sign carried by "Zen Queens." Northampton, Massachusetts was represented by a gigantic purple banner, claiming, "Northampton: Occupied Lesbian Territory." The truly moving sight of hundreds of gay military personnel in uniform and thousands of gay veterans was spiced by a man in full military regalia—and bright red high heels.

Through it all thousands of gay flags flew with our insignia, the rainbow colors, a gorgeous symbol of our joy and diversity. The "Sisters of Perpetual Indulgence," outfitted in their nunly garb, wandered among the crowd. And sprinkled throughout, placards read, "Straight but not Narrow," showing that even our allies picked up our *joie de vivre*.

The constant spoofing of sex roles is a wonderfully healthy and delightful part of gay life. As this society debates the roles of women in the military and in civilian life it may well turn to gays and lesbians, who have long had to figure out who does what based on interest and ability, not gender. We may, indeed, be the clearest representation of the future in our wide-spectrum androgyny. We bend the rules and push the edges, expanding what is possible.

In my house, when my longtime partner asks, "Who is taking out the garbage tonight?" I sometimes reply, "I am, I'm the *man*." Strut and giggle (all the funnier with my femmy appearance).

We are indeed "just like you." With a little some-thing extra added. Maybe because we've been on the outside looking in for so long, we have a clearer view of the party than those who have stood at the center of it. Maybe God knew we were going to have a rocky road, so She gave us an extra dollop of humor. And if there is a gay gene, it's a gene for fun.

In order to form a vision of all of life's possibilities, we need all of our perspectives—including our various senses of humor.

Remember the story of the four blindfolded people who encountered an elephant for the first time? They each felt a part of it, seeking to understand its contours.

"This is a beast which is like a tree trunk," said one, touching the elephant's leg.

"No, it's more like a hose, with a wide entrance," said the one holding the trunk."

"It's definitely flat and wide," said the person feeling the sides of the animal.

"No, it's a thin, ropelike creature," said the one gripping the tail."

Well, put all of those opinions together and . . . we begin to get an accurate representation of an elephant.

As our future folds into our present, more of us will notice the value added when people with a wide variety of perspectives participate in workplaces, schools, social arenas, and neighborhoods. We will see an increasing focus on *valuing* inclusion, rather than dutifully toting up our numbers.

It's an exciting future as we move along the inclusion continuum, heading toward the time when we all sit down together at the welcome table. We'll be dazzled by solutions we'd never considered for our old problems, and delighted by new images. It's a future that is on its way, a future in which history blends with herstory and theirstory to truly become *our* story.

A portion of the proceeds from this book will go to Equity Institute, Inc.

Equity Institute is a multicultural, national non-profit agency, committed to the elimination of all "isms." Founded in 1982, Equity was one of the first non-profit organizations dedicated exclusively to organizational diversity change.

Since its inception, Equity Institute has been on the cutting edge of diversity leadership. With very little capital funding, the Institute has grown to become a national organization which has served more than 100,000 people and 1,000 organizations. Client agencies include large corporations, higher educational institutions, health care organizations, police departments, public schools, and municipal, state and federal government agencies.

The Public Service Program Division provides an opportunity for representatives of community organizations to attend diversity training programs for a nominal fee. These programs are supported by individual contributions, corporate and foundation grants, and revenue from the Client Program Division. Public Service Programs are offered on a regular schedule in four regions of the United States:

MULTICULTURAL LEADERSHIP DEVELOP-
MENT: for community leaders.

PROJECT EMPOWERMENT: for gay/lesbian public
school educators (K-12)

APPRECIATING DIVERSITY: a bi-lingual video-cur-
riculum on homophobia/heterosexism, "Sticks, Stones
and Stereotypes/*Palos, Piedras y Estereotipos*," designed
for educators and young people (grades 7-12).

DISMANTLING RACISM: a program for everyone
concerned about racism.

PROGRAM ON JEWISH AWARENESS: a program
for clergy and community leaders.

DISMANTLING CLASSISM: an intensive program
for community, regional and national leaders in business and social change.

NEW DIRECTIONS IN DIVERSITY: a one-day intro-
ductory program presenting cutting-edge diversity
strategies for community and business leaders.

TRAINING OF TRAINERS: a certification program
teaching the Equity Institute Program Model; organizational diversity assessment, training and technical
assistance, approaches for professional and/or experienced trainers.

CALL OR WRITE EQUITY INSTITUTE FOR MORE
INFORMATION: Equity Institute, Inc., 6400 Hollis
Street, Suite 15, Emeryville, CA 94608, 510-658-4577.